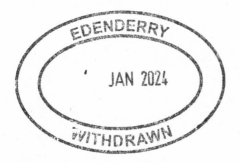

D1355484

Praise for Patrick McGinley

'An imaginative, expertly turned dark comedy, informed by some splendid dialogue and a sensual feel for the claims of the soil.' – *New York Times*

'Patrick McGinley's gifts for resonant dialogue, sexual frictions, graphic violence, and peripeteia have been well noted for over three decades by readers and critics who relish the extravagances of getting lost beyond the Pale.' – *Times Literary Supplement*

'If ever proof was needed that art is not a meritocracy, and success relies more on luck than talent, you'll find it in Patrick McGinley's *Bogmail*. First published in 1978, reissued by New Island, this is not just a great crime novel but a great work of literature.' – *Irish Independent*

'Patrick McGinley is a very gifted man. He knows his Irish bog as well as Isaac Bashevis Singer does the shtetl, and he can sing about it with something like the same magic.' – *New York Times*

'A perceptive, upmarket memoir, rich in exact recall and with ambition to social history.' – *The Irish Times*

'Mr McGinley is inventive and eloquent, his humour puckish and Paddy-wry; he has a fine command of comic irony ... and his evocations of landscape and seascape are successful, not simply as description, but as definitions of a mythic environment.' *London Review of Books*

'A rich and loving novel, *Bogmail* is full of wonder' – *New York Magazine*

Bishop's Delight

A Novel

Patrick McGinley

NEW ISLAND

BISHOP'S DELIGHT
First published in 2016
by
New Island Books,
16 Priory Hall Office Park,
Stillorgan,
County Dublin.
Republic of Ireland.

www.newisland.ie

PRINT ISBN: 978-1-84840-491-5
EPUB ISBN: 978-1-84840-492-2
MOBI ISBN: 978-1-84840-493-9

British Library Cataloguing Data.
A CIP catalogue record for this book is available from the British Library.

Typeset by JVR Creative India
Cover design by Mariel Deegan
Printed by ScandBook AB

New Island received financial assistance from The Arts Council (*An Chomhairle Ealaíon*), 70 Merrion Square, Dublin 2, Ireland.

10 9 8 7 6 5 4 3 2 1

For
Mary and Howard

1

The two joggers slowed down as they came within sight of a seat under a beech tree. In making for it they overtook a pensioner on a stick who'd had the same idea. The shorter of the two flopped down on the seat and pulled a bottle of water from his belt. The tall one watched him drink.

'You're puffed, Bill,' he said, sitting down next to his friend.

With legs outstretched, they observed the other joggers and walkers in silence. The park was a gift from a more spacious time; they met here for a jog once a week, and sometimes the taller of the two came alone because he set store by solitude. Approaching his fifty-eighth birthday, he still could be mistaken for a younger man. He had a full head of steel-grey hair, and he was inclined to think that, like his hero, Charles de Gaulle, he retained a military bearing. In looks he did not in the least resemble de Gaulle: his face was lean, the taut skin pale, and the eyes narrow and piercing. It was not the face of a man who could ever have been mistaken for a matinee idol. His porky friend was red-faced, and with his left bow leg cut a clumsy figure while jogging. They had known each other for over twenty years, and they helped each other when either needed help, as you would expect from close friends.

'I came here for a stroll on Wednesday afternoon,' the tall one said. 'As I was passing a bench, a man with a dog waved to me and said, "Will you come and talk to me?" He turned out to be the most boring man I'd ever met. His conversation was a series of questions to which only he knew the answers. His first question was, "What is the area of this park in Irish acres?" and his next was, "Who first made soda water as a manufactured product?" Who else but a Dubliner called Augustine Thwaites in 1776, or so he claimed.'

'And now you're telling me, Jim!' the porky man laughed. 'Never talk to strange men. That's what my mother told me as a boy.'

'The quiz was only the start of it. He said he'd been hearing terrible stories about goings-on in government. "Everyone knows there's a scandal brewing. There's a new rumour every day of the week. What I'd like to know is where they're all coming from." '

'What did you say?'

'There will always be rumours. It's the nature of democracy, the nature of party politics.'

'I'm sure he must have recognised you.'

'I don't think so. He wasn't the cheeky sort, but in case my speaking voice might give me away, I thanked him for an interesting conversation and made my escape.'

'Rumours come and go. I don't pay any heed to them.'

'These are different, Bill. They're too close to the bone for comfort.'

'There's a libel law in the land. They wouldn't dare publish what I've heard.'

'Don't you believe it. The age of decorum is dead. Modern journalists are happiest dishing the dirt. All they're interested in is sex and scandal—and whatever someone somewhere doesn't want to see published.'

'While readers pay money to read trash, journalists will write it. We're all part of the same vicious circle.'

'It's their high moral tone that gets me. The gutter journalists dig the dirt and the so-called serious journalists hold their noses and rehash the dirt the gutter journalists have already dished.'

'We've both been here before. It will blow over.'

'This time it's different. I've even heard talk of photos. In the popular imagination, photos don't lie.'

'In these days of computers they can and do. Every problem has a price tag. Surely you're not worried about the cost?'

'What I'm worried about is my reputation, my political legacy.'

'Your place in history! You may as well say it. What you need is a few quiet days to get things back in perspective. When life gets too much for me, I go down the country to do some hillwalking on my own. A day in the open is the best panacea I know. I come back to the village in the evening with my tongue hanging out for a pint. My father used to say, "There's no ailment in life that a touch of nature can't cure." He was right.'

'I might just take your advice. I need a few days to myself, looking at the sea and the sky with the mountains somewhere in the background. Do you ever feel used— soiled, I mean—as if you'd been looked at by too many beady eyes?'

'I may feel used at times, but not because too many people have been trying to catch my eye. You're a lucky man, Jim. You're the centre of attention wherever you go.'

'And you're the only person I can talk to. Anna is away with the fairies, writing her children's books and preparing talks for radio. If it weren't for you, I'd go mad.'

'We all need a sympathetic ear, a listener rather than a lecturer. Why don't we do some sleuthing, investigate the source of the leaks?'

'Too risky. In fact, it's occurred to me that we should give up our Thursday jog. Anything that attracts the attention of cartoonists soon becomes a caricature of itself.'

'I don't suppose you've thought of retiring? Quitting while you're ahead?'

'There's nothing the young Turks in the party would like better. In the past year I've seen off two attempts at a coup. The word "quit" isn't in my vocabulary. No, I'll stay and face whatever music is to be faced. I'm a fighter, not a quitter. Always do the unexpected. It's the way to confound the enemy.'

The porky man got to his feet. He had obviously heard it all before. 'I must be getting back,' he said. 'I'm taking Maggie out to dinner. It's my way of keeping her happy.'

'Dinner always works wonders. Whenever Anna feels unappreciated, I whisk her out of the kitchen. Wives are precious, but they need pampering to keep them from asking awkward questions.'

2

What other journalists wrote was only for the day; what Kevin Woody was writing was for posterity, or so he liked to tell himself. To keep body and soul together he had to write some things for the day, of course, but every evening he returned to his lonely house in Drumcondra to commit to paper the words that would give weight and substance to his magnum opus: the biography no one knew he was writing. He had spent the last ten years writing and rewriting, adding a paragraph here and deleting a sentence there; now all he was waiting for was the ending. For that he must outlive his subject, a requirement he sought to fulfil by taking good care of himself. He didn't overeat, and unlike some of the other hacks he knew, he did not drink himself into a stupor every night of the week. Though he stood over six foot tall in his socks, he weighed only twelve stone four before breakfast. He went for a walk in the park from time to time and pumped iron at the gym once a week. For a man in his forty-ninth year he was in good shape, and, equally important, his mind was as sharp as ever.

His subject was none other than the Taoiseach himself, the battle-scarred Jim Maguire. He had been leader of his party for seventeen years, and Taoiseach for four terms in the coalition governments he was so good at putting together. He was now fifty-seven, eight years older than Woody, and in less than perfect health. It was rumoured that he had a mild heart condition. Last year he was admitted to hospital with arrhythmia, only to be released again after two days. Still, no one really knew the minute or the hour. It was rather exciting. You could say that all he was waiting for was the bellman's signal to write the final appraisal. Meanwhile, he would carry on honing and making perfect.

His book, which he had provisionally called *Political Magpie* in acknowledgement of Maguire's predatory and idea-thieving nature, was no common or garden biography. He had taken as his model Lytton Strachey's *Eminent Victorians*, and nothing would convince him that he himself had not set an even higher benchmark in acerbic wit and stylishness. Although it was no part of his ambition to perpetuate Maguire's memory, he felt certain that his book would be read for its literary grace long after its subject was forgotten.

He had known Maguire at university. They shared digs and went everywhere together. A mature student because of a polio setback, Maguire was stimulating company. He was reading history and French, but even then everyone knew that his future lay in politics. He was an accomplished mimic, a witty and resourceful debater, and a keen supporter of what more radical students saw as the Crooks' Party. Some even joked that Maguire, like Milton, belonged to the Devil's Party without knowing it. Not that Maguire cared. He was impervious to the jibes of lesser men; he used to say that a thick skin was the best legacy anyone could have from his parents.

After graduating, he and Maguire founded and edited a political monthly from a small basement office in Nassau Street, but from the start he could see that Maguire's sights were set on higher things. He had been selected to contest his father's old seat in East Mayo on behalf of the Crooks' Party, which naturally their magazine supported. Then, in the midst of rejoicing, disaster struck. Their magazine was sued for malicious libel, and there was no money in the kitty to defend the case against them. After weeks of hard bargaining they settled out of court, which cost Woody every penny of his savings. Maguire said he needed whatever funds he had to fight the election. In coming to his rescue, Woody wasn't being entirely selfless: he had told Maguire that the price he must pay for having his political life saved was to stay away from Anna Harvey, their attractive young secretary. Within weeks, the magazine folded. Maguire was elected to the Dáil, while Woody found himself jobless and penniless. Unbeknown to him, Maguire was still seeing Anna. They got married the following year.

He was badly bruised by Maguire's perfidy, but he did not let Maguire or Anna see it. They invited him to their wedding, and he accepted their invitation. He even bought them a present he could ill afford. It was all part of his plan; he was in no hurry, he was playing a waiting game. Maguire's career blossomed while Woody did his best to get by on a slender income derived from political journalism and occasional book reviewing. Though a bond of trust had been broken, he and Maguire still met for drinks because it was in the interest of both of them to keep the lines of communication open. Maguire found him useful when he wished to discuss a new policy or plant the germ of an idea in the public domain that would later blossom to the detriment of a political rival. Woody was more than willing to fall into his prescribed role because he was often the first recipient of the titbits that fell from Maguire's table. In time he came to be respected by his colleagues for his prescience and confident analysis of complex political issues. He knew that he was being used, but still he smiled, telling himself that revenge is a dish best served cold.

Today he wasn't thinking of Maguire. Instead, he was wondering why Tony Sweetman had phoned him with such urgency. They were in the habit of meeting every Friday to make what Sweetman in his uninspired way described as 'an early start on the weekend'. Sweetman was a TV journalist, good for the memorable sound bite, the cocktail sausage and the canapé as opposed to a solid three-course dinner. He was a tireless networker; he knew everyone and trusted no one, and as a consequence no one trusted him. It was only Tuesday, so what was on his mind that could not wait till Friday? He wouldn't show any curiosity. He would be his usual cool-headed, slow-spoken self.

They met upstairs in Neary's because it suited their pockets and because it wasn't a haunt of their fellow hacks. Sweetman had already arrived, looking his usual suspicious self, turning his head and stretching his neck like a vigilant cormorant on a rock. He was the type of man who was at his best on television. An envious colleague once observed that he never relaxed except in front of the cameras. Now he was seated at the corner table with his back to the window and the light. He was reading a paperback, which he slipped into his briefcase the moment Woody appeared at the door.

'Reading something sexy?'

'If only. I'm ploughing through a biography of de Gaulle. I'm just curious to know what Maguire can see in the cold-blooded old Froggy. They say he knows by heart every last one of de Gaulle's *bons mots*.'

When they'd ordered lunch and settled down to their drinks, Sweetman gave him a long look of cool appraisal. 'When did you last see Maguire?' he whispered, leaning forward conspiratorially in his chair.

'Just over a week ago. He was his usual urbane and blasé self.'

'When are you meeting him again?'

'I don't make dates with Maguire. His secretary rings me. The traffic is all one way. It could be months before I see him on his own again.'

'A week, never mind a month, is a long time in politics, as another old twister once said. I'll bet he won't be as blasé next time. There's a raincloud on the horizon that could drench him. I've had it from a little bird who had it from a bigger bird who shall be nameless. I thought I'd tip you the wink. It's no more than you'd do for me.'

Sweetman actually winked at him as if he knew more than he was letting on. The purpose of the meeting had finally become apparent; he wanted to find out if Woody knew something he himself didn't know. Woody thought it time to cast a few crumbs on the water to see what might rise to the bait.

'We live in a world of rumours. I've heard one as well,' he said.

'Can we both have heard the same rumour, do you think?'

'It's all too possible.'

Sweetman looked around the room as if to establish whether anyone was eavesdropping on their conversation.

'You can't be too careful,' he said, pulling out a little notebook from an inner pocket. Removing a page, which he tore in two, he pushed one half in Woody's direction and kept the other half himself. 'We'll each write just two words about the rumour we've heard. We'll exchange papers. That way no word will be spoken and no word overheard.'

Woody took a thin little pencil from his pocket diary and wrote two words. Sweetman extracted a biro from his jacket and also wrote two words, then pushed his scrap in Woody's direction. Woody reciprocated and turned up Sweetman's paper, on which the words 'KINKY SEX' were written in block capitals. He had written the words 'BIG MONEY' on his scrap.

'We've heard different stories,' Sweetman said, with an air of disappointment.

'Not necessarily. We may have heard different facets of the same story.'

'Money and sex, horse and cart. Now we'll both be on the alert. Knowing what you're looking for is half the battle. Share and share alike has always been my philosophy.'

After they'd eaten, they shared the bill before going their separate ways, Woody somewhat nonplussed and Sweetman with a spring in his step. He didn't know what to make of Sweetman. Some said he was a bit naïve; others that the naïvety was a mask to mislead the unwary. He was troubled by the words Sweetman had written. Kinky sex was the last thing he would have associated with Maguire. Everyone knew of his interest in big money and in the kind of people who possessed it. He contrived to live in style. He had a mansion in Howth, a fine house in Mayo, and a desirable little cottage in Conamara. He owned two racehorses and a yacht in Howth Harbour for the entertainment of his cronies. In writing BIG MONEY he was giving nothing away. But why did Sweetman write KINKY SEX? Did he really know something, or was he chancing his arm to see how he'd react? No matter how he looked at it, it was worrying. If there was anything in the story, it would upset the balance of his book. He had portrayed Maguire as an ice-cold puritan whose only weakness was the love of money and moneybags. He would have to keep his ear to the ground. It was too early to write the last chapter. To use the time-honoured metaphor, the fat lady had yet to sing.

On the way home he paused outside what used to be the Pearl Bar, recalling the unswept floor, the hard benches, the grubby windows whose filtered light changed the colour of her wavy brown hair. They used to meet there after work. He still thought of her as Anna Harvey; he couldn't bear to think of her as Anna Maguire. She was young then, no more than twenty. He had a photo of her leaning against a tree in the green. She wore a pale green blouse and purple dress that summer because, she said, everyone else was wearing white and pink. Again he heard her laugh: 'I'm amused when shop assistants say, "Green doesn't go with purple." They don't seem to understand. A friend of mine has a cat she calls Macavity. When I suggested she call him MacAlister instead, she told me to read T. S. Eliot. Some people are dull beyond belief.' He had loved her then; he was young enough to see the city and the world through her eyes.

In O'Connell Street he turned a corner, seeking unavailingly the entrance to the vanished Prince's Bar. It was long and narrow, so they used to meet in the far end, the Holy of Holies, as she called it. She liked talking to the old barman who came from Toomevara. Once when he happened to be late he found her on a high stool at the bar smiling at the barman's stories of the turf. He had given her what he called a certainty. She put a bob each way on Jeroboam, and collected nineteen shillings and eight pence. That evening she went back to the Prince's and bought the barman a large Jameson. That's what she was like before she married Maguire, a girl of verve and sparkle, ready to act on impulse no matter how. At times he used to wonder what she'd come up with next. How could she have allowed it to happen, the long, sad dwindling into mediocrity? She was totally under his thumb. Maguire liked to think of himself as a great leader, a modern Dev without Dev's blind spots, and of course he convinced her to begin writing stories for children like her predecessor, Sinéad, who had stayed obediently at home, enduring without complaint the great man's icy demeanour. He decided to walk home because he liked walking and because he wanted to empty his mind of all memories of his meeting with Sweetman.

Just in time he remembered that he was supposed to be meeting Jane at five-thirty. She came straight from work, the picture of brisk efficiency. She worked for a firm of solicitors; what else could you expect? He told her she looked stunning because she liked to be reassured. The pub was quiet; the barbarians hadn't yet arrived. There was an old couple across from them who were staring blankly into space. A young couple on the right were having an argument.

'Would you rather be the silent old pair or the young hotheads?' she asked.

'Neither, I'm happy as I am.'

'I think it's time we got married,' she said, for the tenth time that month. She said it at least twice, and sometimes three times a week.

'You have no idea of the precarious state of my finances. I can barely support myself, let alone the two of us.'

'I wouldn't be a millstone round your neck. I'd bring home my share of the bacon. I could sell my flat. Your house is big enough for both of us.'

'Property values are going down. It isn't a good time to sell unless you're buying as well.'

'You're never without an excuse, Woody.'

'Trust me. I know what I'm doing. I've got something on the boil that could land us both in clover.'

'Are you planning to win the lottery?'

'I'm not stupid. I don't do the lottery.'

'Just think if you won the jackpot! What would you do with it?'

'I'd take you on a cruise round the world. We'd have a whirlwind romance in the Roaring Forties and we'd get married in Tahiti, and I'd put a garland of flowers around your neck.'

'You can never be serious. You haven't got one serious thought in that high head of yours.'

'I'm so serious that I've come full circle. The only thing in this ludicrous world I'm serious about is you.'

'So when are we getting married then?'

'We'll get married when we're both in step, without one bone of contention between us.'

'What you're saying is, "Stop chuntering, Jane." Is that it?'

'We'll talk at the weekend. I've got a lot on my mind at the moment.'

'What are you thinking about now?'

'I was thinking that the inside of this pub looks like the interior of a church.'

'There are times when I think you're quite mad, Woody.'

'I'm not mad. You see, the craftsmen who worked on the interior of the Dublin churches also did the furnishings of the old Dublin pubs. Look at those benches and the stained-glass windows.'

'We'll never get married at this rate,' she said.

He reached for her hand. 'Put today's date in your diary. We'll be married before it comes around again next year.'

3

Anna Maguire was enjoying a few quiet days on her own. Jim had gone to the cottage for a short break 'to fish mackerel and think about things.' He enjoyed rock fishing, but he also had a rowboat with an outboard for those quiet times when he wanted to be alone on the water. As a rule there was no one more gregarious than Jim. He loved good company and the cut and thrust of after-dinner conversation, but he often told her that solitude was the greatest luxury in his life and his greatest temptation. Politics was a bruising business. After a week in Kildare Street he needed a few days among rocks and sheep and seagulls to recover his natural bounce and eagerness for the battle.

He wouldn't mind having to fend for himself at the cottage. A countryman born and bred, he wasn't the helpless type; he would be glad of the opportunity to fish for his supper and then cook whatever he'd caught. He could fry a mackerel, boil a few potatoes and carrots or roast some parsnips, his favourite vegetable. One way or another he wouldn't go hungry; she had packed a few tins of this and that to tide him over in case the sea was rough. She had offered to go with him, and she was pleased when he said that he didn't want to take her away from her writing. She was putting the finishing touches to a talk she was giving to the ICA, and she needed to do some shopping in advance of the book launch on Thursday. Still, she couldn't help being worried about him. There was something on his mind that he hadn't shared with her. She knew him well enough to read the signs.

He used to say that 'the politician who loses touch with his public is like an actor who doesn't know when the play is over. It happens eventually to the best us. It happened to Dev and de Gaulle. In England it happened to Churchill and Thatcher. It won't happen to me,' he'd promised her more than once. 'When my time is up, I won't hang about. I'll take rock fishing and cooking seriously.'

She advised him to give up while he was still on top, but like all politicians he was headstrong. 'No, I'd like to win one last election outright, and hand over to the young Turks six months later. I'm not power-mad; power is a Dead Sea fruit, as that old fox Harold Macmillan once said. It's ashes in the mouth once you've achieved it.'

If he had a weakness as a politician, it lay in his readiness to please journalists. He saw them as the connecting rod between him and the man in the street, the man in the drain, the man on the tractor, and the housewife doing the weekend shopping. He himself had begun his career as a journalist, and he still retained his ear for the colourful metaphor, the journalistic aphorism. He had divided journalists into two camps: those whose weapon is aggressive probing, and those who seek the Achilles heel by subtle flattery. Though wary of both, he never turned down an opportunity to pit his wits against either. He had his favourites, of course. Among the flatterers, he had a soft spot for Kevin Woody, and among the gladiators he respected Tony Sweetman for his slithery subtlety. 'You needn't worry,' he'd said to her. 'I can handle both. All a politician needs to know about hacks is that the best story wins. They're only entertainers who've wrapped themselves in the flag of truth. No sense of history. No scale of values. The rise of an eagle and the fall of a sparrow are one and the same to them. There will always be another and a better story tomorrow.'

She had her own views. She could understand his closeness to Kevin Woody, but she questioned his acceptance of the wiles of Sweetman. Kevin Woody was an old friend. They both knew him. After all, it was Woody who'd brought them together. He was an odd man out among journalists. He had few friends, which was probably why Jim trusted him.

Jim himself wasn't a typical politician, if only because he didn't rate politics highly; he saw it as a debased pursuit, unworthy of a man with a really serious cast of mind. 'What kind of man enjoys answering questions about the failure of the water pump in Ballyhuppachaun one day and rising unemployment and interest rates the next?' I'm a politician because I have a second-rate mind. If I had a good mind I'd have devoted my life to enlarging the sum total of human knowledge.'

He was disappointed in his political career. Somehow or other he felt that the Irish people never quite saw him as one of themselves. 'They respected me, but they didn't trust me. They made my party the largest party, but they never gave me an overall majority. They condemned me to a life of wheeling and dealing, going cap in hand to lesser parties and lesser men. It was as if they wanted to teach me a lesson in case I got too big for my boots.'

She tried to reason with him to make him see the bright side. She told him that politics in a democracy was ultimately about persuasion, which was what he was good at. 'So you see me as a salesman! I can only agree with you. Like all politicians, a salesman of other people's ideas. Name me one politician anywhere with an original mind.'

In one of his depressive moods he was unreachable, but fortunately such moods were rare. She would listen and sympathise, which was all he needed. He didn't expect reasoned argument from her; he loved her because of her willingness to understand. She knew he'd had affairs, but none of them had lasted. He was conservative in his tastes, and he needed a woman in the same mould.

When they first got married, she'd had no idea of the kind of life they'd lead. He was a newly elected TD; he had yet to make his mark. She'd told him not to expect her to become a typical politician's wife, and he said that one politician in any family was enough. They entertained from time to time, but not lavishly, mainly friends they both happened to know. As they didn't have children, she was free to give her time to writing and amateur dramatics. He was busy with his meetings; some weeks she saw very little of him in the evenings. If it hadn't been for the house in his Mayo constituency and the weekend cottage in Galway, they'd have lived separate lives. Yet his shadow was all over the house, even while he was absent. Wherever she went, she was seen as the Taoiseach's wife. Whenever she published a book, he would come to the launch party, and he would be sure to make a witty speech. At times she wished he'd stay away, but she couldn't bring herself to tell him so. Instead she smiled at his by now familiar jokes and accepted her role without demur. When things became too much, she would tell him that her sister Lily, who lived in Skibbereen, had invited her down for a week. There were even times when she wondered what her life would have been like had she married a less successful man. At such moments she would think of Kevin Woody, who in every respect was Jim's opposite, but somehow she couldn't imagine a life of scrimping and making do. Jim had spoilt her; she had all the comforts any sensible woman could wish for.

She had finished work on her ICA talk. They wouldn't be a difficult audience to please; most of them would come in the hope that she might let slip a comment or two on life with the man himself. In the afternoon she went shopping in Grafton Street, taking care to dress inconspicuously so as not to draw attention to herself. As she came out of Brown Thomas she spotted Kevin Woody on the other side of the street. He had his back to her. With his hands deep in his trousers pockets he looked hunched and self-absorbed. Hoping he had not seen her, she slipped into Bewley's for a cup of tea and a currant bun. He obviously had seen her. She had barely had time to order when he came stalking in and nodded in what seemed like surprised recognition.

'Lovely to see you, Anna. Mind if I join you?'

What could she say except, 'Please do.' Journalists were masters of the hackneyed phrase, and they had the knack of bringing out the hackneyed phrase in everyone else as well.

He said he had just bought a CD to celebrate an unexpected cheque, and he asked her if she would join him for a drink in Enright's. At first she was somewhat surprised, but the prospect of going to a pub again made her think twice.

'Where is Enright's?' she asked, playing for time.

'It's off Anne Street. It's a quiet place; no one else goes there. I thought you mightn't like to be seen boozing with a common hack.'

She couldn't help laughing. 'You're an old friend, Kevin. Not many of the people I know go back as far. It must be over fifteen years since I was last in a pub. It will bring back memories.'

The lunchtime drinkers had returned to work. Enright's was almost empty. They found a table under a stained-glass window, and he got her a spritzer and a pint of Guinness for himself. He was lively and amusing, telling her stories about other journalists whose names she'd heard but whose faces she would not recognise. All the time she kept wondering what was really on his mind. Surely as a journalist he must have had

18

an ulterior motive, but he never once asked her about anything to do with Jim. On the way home she chided herself for having misjudged him. Listening to Jim had made her suspicious of everyone. After all, Kevin was an old friend. Living on his own, he must get lonely. The unexpected cheque was probably a fiction. All he wanted was someone to listen and talk to him to shorten the afternoon.

After dinner she phoned Jim at the cottage. The weather, he said, was cloudy but dry, the sea calm. As she expected, he'd had fried mackerel for dinner, and he was planning to go whiffing from the boat tomorrow in the hope of catching something less oily for a change. He told her he was looking forward to some real home cooking when he got back, and asked what she'd been doing. When he heard that she'd met Kevin Woody in Grafton Street and that he'd invited her for a drink in Enright's there was a silence of two seconds at the other end of the line.

'What was on his mind?' he asked finally.

'He was in a jolly mood, out to celebrate an unexpected cheque.'

'Did he talk politics?'

'Not to me.'

'Did he ask where I was?'

'He never mentioned your name. It wasn't that type of conversation. He was just in a mood for light-hearted gossip, telling stories about the people he knows.'

'You can't be too careful, Anna. Journalists are not what they seem to be, and Woody is no exception.'

'You needn't worry, Jim. I'm nothing if not discreet.'

'Anything interesting in the post?'

'You know I never open your post. I leave that to Jean.'

'I'll drive back Sunday afternoon. I'll be home in time for dinner. There's something on television I'd like to see.'

As she put down the phone, she caught a glimpse of herself in the mirror. The look on her face was introspective. She was worried about Jim. There was something on his mind that he did not want her to know. He knew perfectly well that she never opened his post. His official post went to his office. All that came to the house was personal correspondence, household bills and the usual junk mail. She switched on the television, but she couldn't concentrate. Her mind was filled with thoughts of Jim.

4

Tony Sweetman was deep in thought, in two minds as to what to do. He was writing a biography of Maguire on the quiet, and he had just heard by the merest chance that his sparring companion, Kevin Woody, was engaged in the same surreptitious pursuit. Maguire was an old friend of Woody, and had quite possibly given Woody access to his files. Woody was not an open man. He worked in the shadows; he liked to spring a surprise. Woody's biography would be well received. He was an accomplished journalist and a regular attendee at debates in the Dáil. What he didn't know about the workings of parliament wasn't worth knowing. His biography would not be a scissors-and-paste job; it could be a serious threat to his own long-cherished ambitions as a writer. Though held in high esteem as a presenter of current affairs programmes, he was determined to leave behind something more solid than the memory of a handsome face on the box.

Woody was obviously thinking along the same lines. He, too, was unhappy about the ephemerality of daily journalism; he, too, wished for a limited immortality, to be remembered for a decade or two after his death. He could suggest to Woody that they share their sources and even collaborate on the writing of the great work, but Woody was not a team player. All his life he had been a freelance. Even in the pub in the company of his fellow journalists, he never relaxed from his self-appointed role of unsentimental observer. Curiously, he was well liked, even respected by those who mattered. He was never in anyone's way, never presenting a threat to a more ambitious colleague or a younger man on the make. That in fact was his secret. He himself might do well to cultivate a similarly ambiguous strategy.

If only he could muddy the waters in which Maguire and Woody swam! If only he could get Woody to write something that reflected badly on Maguire. Woody was no arse-licker; he was a serious journalist whose head might be turned by the possibility of a scoop. Illumination came with the speed of a bullet from a rifle. He would phone Woody and suggest a quick lunch. 'Quick' would give an impression of urgency, of a story on the point of breaking. They were in the habit of meeting on Fridays. This time he would suggest Thursday to make Woody imagine something that could not wait.

Woody was not lacking in imagination. To make up his mind, he wouldn't need to eat the whole cake. He'd give him a taster, just a crumb or two to sharpen his appetite for a slice. Woody being Woody would suspect an ulterior motive. He was an out-and-out cynic; as a baby he'd probably had doubts about the milk from his mother's breast. Now the sourness of his cynicism as a man could only be neutralised by a deeper and more subtle cynicism, a kind of psychological homeopathy. The first question Woody would ask was, 'Why is this bugger Sweetman offering me a pearl on a plate? And why me? Why not Bantock, Barker or McCabe?' Only then would he consider the merits of the story. That was his Achilles' heel, his obsession with the ulterior motive rather than the likelihood of the events themselves. Lastly, Woody was a loner. He would mull things over by his own cold fireplace, too secretive, too independent to seek confirmation from a friend. For that reason, he wouldn't press him. He would give him the 'facts' and observe his initial reaction. Only then would he follow up with a strategy best suited to counter or encourage his initial response. Given a little forethought and preparation, nothing or next to nothing could go wrong.

As usual, they met upstairs in Neary's, Woody's preferred watering hole. He might join colleagues in their customary pleasure palaces, but when he fancied a quiet drink he always headed for the homely Neary's. Woody was a man of set habits. You could almost predict where to find him at any hour of the day or night. They had arranged to meet at noon. He made sure that he arrived before Woody so that he could observe how he entered and judge from the angle of his stoop and the contour of his lower lip the prevailing mood of the day. He entered with a breezy air: fair stood the wind for a quick conversational spinnaker run over the cold salmon salad.

For a man of his literary exactitude, he was surprisingly careless in his dress. He never wore a tie, and he carried a sagging and shapeless shoulder bag, into which he stuffed an assortment of newspapers, books, magazines and other necessaries, including small items of shopping. He dumped the bulging bag onto a vacant chair and sat facing the bar with his back to the wall.

'What's up?' he asked, running a hand over his ruffled blonde curls.

'First things first. What would you like to drink?'

'A pint of the darkly-go-down, excuse the cliché. It's the only constant in my kaleidoscopic life.'

Having taken his first sip of the day, Woody looked at him expectantly, which was precisely how Sweetman wished to be looked at. He knew that Woody was dying to know what was on his mind, and at the same time he wished to prolong the enjoyment of his position as the repository of a secret so precious that it must on no account be overheard. He looked around the room to make sure that there were no other journalists in the bar.

'We're not spies,' Woody said. 'And I'm sure we're not being spied on. So don't keep me in suspense.'

Again he looked all around, more out of habit than histrionics, after which he told Woody in low conspiratorial tones that a high-class Parisian courtesan had been in touch with him.

'High class? Far too expensive for me,' Woody grinned.

'She wasn't selling her services. She was selling information.'

'Let me guess. The Archbishop stops off for a blowjob in Paris on the way to and from Rome?'

'No, her info was even more sensational. That well-known ascetic Jim Maguire is among her most exacting clients.'

'Did she really use the word "exacting"? Tell the truth.'

'No, she didn't. She used a word that sounded like *exigeant,* but I can't be sure. It seemed to me at the time that she said, *"trop exigeant".'*

'What makes you think she's high class?'

'Her prices, and her way with language. Her English is remarkably good, faultlessly idiomatic but beautifully French. When I asked her where she'd learnt her English, her face lit up. "From my clients", she smiled.'

'How come she knows you?'

'She doesn't. She wants to sell her story, and she asked me straight out if I might be interested.'

'Surely she must know some more likely outlets.'

'She saw me interviewing Emmanuelle Béart on the box and liked my style. She wants to be interviewed by me.'

'Well, what's stopping you?'

'This is a red-hot story, but I'm a bit worried about whether it's reliable. It would be disastrous if it turned out that she's some sort of crank. She sounds a bit of a loose cannon, far too keen to dish the dirt on Maguire. Apparently, he's just pulled the plug on a close relationship over many years. Sex, and lots of it. Kinky sex. Three-in-a-bed sex. Also what Maguire calls "the descent to Nibelheim", which, she says, he likes performing to the appropriate music.'

'You say three in a bed. Two women and one man. His stock will go up. He'll be seen as a true patriot and possibly a true Gael.'

'Not two women and one man: two men and one woman. Sounds a bit kinky to me.'

'And who is the understudy?'

'You know him well. Bill MacBride, Maguire's old buddy and confidant. It's red hot. It will be taken up by all the papers here as well as in England. I thought I'd give you first refusal.'

'If it had happened twenty years ago it would have been a red-hot story. Sex is old hat these days. Everyone is at it, so why not the Taoiseach? No one gives a fiddler's any more.'

'This is different. These days you can have as much sex as you like, *provided you don't pay for it*. This is the business, I'm telling you. She's kept detailed accounts; how much he paid for a blowjob, how much for a back scuttle, and how much for some newfangled Froggy refinement whose name I forget. Believe me, the nomenclature alone is worth the price.'

'So where do I come into this outré menagerie?'

'Unfortunately, she's mercenary. She's only interested in the money—more money than I can get together. That's where you come in. I need someone with time to check the facts, someone with wide contacts. You know every editor in the business both here and in London, you're the obvious man. Without giving too much away, you could find out how much in total her story is worth.'

'And where do you come in?'

'I would hope to get the story for television, once it's been authenticated by you. It would be a feather in my cap and in yours. Besides, she's stunningly good looking with an amusing French lisp. You'll enjoy talking to her, if nothing else.'

'I'll sleep on it and let you know tomorrow.'

As usual, Woody was playing for time. Now he would go back to his gaunt hutch in Drumcondra and stare into his empty fireplace until every conceivable contingency had shuffled in procession past his jaundiced eye. He couldn't think on his feet; that was his problem. He was good for a column on Wednesdays and Sundays. He wouldn't last five minutes in the panic and pandemonium of a TV newsroom. Still, he was nobody's fool. Politicians chose their words carefully when he was around. In an article, but not in live discussion, he was capable of turning the tables by a deft turn of phrase, as one or two cabinet ministers discovered to their cost. Woody was not to be treated lightly. He would have to proceed with caution, making sure to cover his tracks.

5

He did not know what to make of Sweetman's story. Should he take it up in a non-committal way, or should he reject it out of hand? The story itself did not sound altogether implausible. Maguire was a well-known Francophile. He was fluent in French, and he went to Paris more often than was necessary for strictly political purposes. Admittedly, he was interested in French art and French theatre, and he was widely read in French literature. In Paris he would have had ample opportunity in the evenings to explore the more obscure byways of French culture.

His elitist instinct ensured that the Irish electorate had never taken him to their heart of hearts. Everyone knew that he had been born in Mayo, God help us, and no one could work out why he had to lisp like the French. His indifference to the electorate was, of course, a point in his favour. While his political opponents drank Guinness in public and champagne in private, Maguire never deviated either in public or in private from his favourite Volnay, and when no other Baune was on offer he would ask for a glass of spring water instead. This, rather than the Volnay, was what the plain people of Ireland could not understand. Once, at a press reception in a Galway pub, a journalist said to him, 'You're not drinking the good Guinness, I see.' Maguire smiled down at him and said, 'I'm drinking the good water instead. Adam's ale versus Arthur's ale.

De gustibus non disputandum.' Needless to say, the journalist was quick to make capital of the comment. He explained to his readers the following Sunday that Maguire had put him down with a well-worn Latin tag in a comment he could just as easily have made in plain English: 'There's no disputing tastes.' Maguire despised journalists, and not without reason. It was ignorant journalists who had given currency to the general notion that he was an incorrigible snob.

None of that, of course, was relevant to Woody's response to Sweetman's offer. If he took it up he would be risking Maguire's friendship, coming out in the open as an ally of Sweetman and the rest of the baying pack. But if he didn't take it up someone else would, leaving him sidelined without access to the story of the day, a story that was bound to run for weeks and weeks. Still, Maguire's trust and friendship was too precious to put at risk. On it depended the success of his ambition to write the definitive biography. But there was a third course: he could warn Maguire about the machinations of his enemies and earn his heartfelt gratitude. That was the course he proposed to follow. He would phone Maguire's office tomorrow and mention 'Barna', a code word he had used several times before. Maguire would know that something was in the air; he would phone back or at least send him a text before the morning was out. One way or another he would have an answer before his lunch with Sweetman on Friday.

In the excitement of the moment he had forgotten that he must eat. Jane had wanted to come and cook him dinner, but he had put her off with an excuse she could not but accept. He opened his shoulder bag and, after rummaging among the papers and books, found two smoked trout fillets, a pot of coleslaw and potato salad, a pot of Moroccan couscous and a small jar of horseradish sauce. After his encounter with Sweetman he fancied a quiet evening on his own. He would stretch out on the sofa and listen to some Bach, the *Goldberg Variations* and one or two motets, allowing random thoughts to float in and out of his mind. Being silent was his way of being creative, whereas Jane's way was to engage in the kind of combative conversation that found resolution only between the sheets.

He was fond of Jane. Like him, she had never married, and they had been friends for nearly ten years. She could look pretty when she took trouble with her hair, which wasn't all the time. Her great failing was her too-obvious eagerness for matrimony 'before it is too late'. Most of their wrangling and occasional fallings-out had to do with his reluctance to buy her an engagement ring.

'Is there someone else?' she would demand out of the blue.

'Of course there isn't,' he would say.

'Then what's the problem?'

'I'm an old-fashioned bachelor. I'm not the marrying type.'

'I won't give up. I'll give you no peace. I'll lead you to the altar even if I have to put a ring in your nose.'

The prospect did not deter him entirely. It was something he knew he might conceivably do when the time was ripe. She was twelve years younger than he, but by several other systems of reckoning she was twelve years older. She had a ready opinion on everything, whereas most of the time he had to rack his brains to come up with an opinion he could call his own. It was a constant battle of wits. She demanded the kind of conversation that made sparks fly. Ideally, he'd like a girl who could amuse herself during the day and leave him to his own devices until it was time for bed. If he married Jane, he'd never have a moment's peace.

He sat down to his cold dinner, and, having masticated the first mouthful of smoked trout, said aloud to himself, 'Sweetman's story stinks. I reckon he's having me on.' An hour later he fell asleep on the sofa and woke at midnight fully rested. He read two ghost stories by M. R. James and went to bed in the small hours in a mood of blissful contentment. The radio roused him from a dream. He imagined he'd heard someone say that the Taoiseach Jim Maguire had been reported missing. 'He went fishing alone in his rowboat off the Conamara coast yesterday morning and hasn't returned. A search is now in progress and further news is expected at any moment.' In spite of having heard, he still wasn't certain that he'd heard what he thought he heard. He took the radio to the bathroom and shaved as he waited for the next news bulletin. He phoned one or two journalist friends, but they knew no more than he'd already gleaned. Enlightenment finally came two hours later. Maguire's boat had been found drifting two miles off the coast with no oars and no petrol in the outboard tank. No trace of Maguire had been found, and the search for a body was still going on.

He phoned Sweetman, only to find that he was already on his way to the scene of the action. He phoned Jane and told her that he was going to drive over to Conamara to talk to the locals and see for himself how the tragedy could have happened.

'Does that put the tin hat on our Sunday lunch?' she asked.

'I would hope not. I'll be writing a think-piece for your favourite Sunday paper. I plan to get back Saturday afternoon at the very latest.'

That seemed to placate her, at least for the moment. She always cooked his Sunday lunch, invariably roast beef or lamb, which they washed down with a bottle of supermarket claret. After lunch they would go to bed for the afternoon, and after bed they would do the washing-up together and spend an hour or two watching a film on television until it was time for her to go home. Sunday, he used to tell himself, was the trickiest day of the week, a day when he had to mind his every word, because if all didn't go well the memory of discord would colour his thoughts for the rest of the week.

On arrival in Inverrone village the first person he met was Sweetman, who took him aside and revealed that this was not a drowning accident, far from it: it smelt of dirty work, and what is more the dirty work of a well-known third party.

'And who might that party be, I wonder?' Woody thought he'd try gentle sarcasm.

'Ask yourself which party has been against law and order in this country since the foundation of the State, and you'll have your answer.'

'You're a born conspirator, Sweetman. You think and speak in riddles.'

'I'll give you a little hint. Maguire was at the forefront of the Northern Ireland negotiations with the Brits. There are those who see him as a forelock-tugging Anglophile, those who think he sold the pass.'

'What nonsense!'

'No, don't say a word.' Sweetman put a forefinger to his lips. 'Just give your imagination time to dwell on it. I didn't make all this up. I have my ear to the ground and a wet finger to the wind. All I'm doing is giving you a little hint of the way the wind is blowing.'

'So you think Maguire was seized from his boat and the boat left to drift?'

'I think he's now at the bottom of some lough with stones in his pockets and a bullet in the back of his neck. It's what these barbarians do, isn't it?'

'Where is your evidence?'

'Evidence?! We don't need evidence. People expect life to have a plot like a novel, and they know that the aim of any murderer is to leave no trace behind. The greater the mystery the easier it is to believe in a conspiracy. Maguire led a very private life. He's left us a clean slate to write on. It's the opportunity of a lifetime; we can write and say whatever we like.'

'You can hardly air those views on the telly.'

'Don't worry. I know what I'm doing. I know how to prepare the ground.'

'What about your courtesan? Have you forgotten her?'

'I've been trying to get hold of her but she's incommunicado. What does that suggest to you?'

'She's in bed with a richer punter?'

'Wrong again. She realised that what happened to Maguire could well happen to her. She's gone to ground, not bed.'

Sweetman raised a forefinger and tapped his temple. 'In this business it helps to stay one leap ahead of the posse.'

He wished Sweetman the best of luck in his investigations and headed for the nearest pub. He had an article to write, and with any luck he might meet a wiseacre or two with a gift for colourful gossip. He didn't have far to look. Soon he had joined four men at the bar, who were determined to educate him in the saga of Maguire's meanness with money. They even had their own name for him, 'Spume', in acknowledgement of the fact that he was the first to use the word in that part of the world. He could tell that they enjoyed talking about Maguire. They admitted that he was friendly but still kept his distance. One man said he was 'as tight as tuppence in a rag'; that unlike the tourists he never employed a local boatman. He had his own boat, and he went out in her alone in all weathers. An old man called Fergus explained that he wasn't really tight; that he just liked doing things on his own. 'Some men are like that,' he added. 'They can't help it. It's the way they are.'

'Spume was full of notions about himself,' another man said. 'He wouldn't speak to you unless you spoke first.'

'Well, I was probably the last man he spoke to,' Fergus said. 'I was mending a net for Páidín on the pier when down he came with his canvas rucksack and two oars on his shoulder. It was the same bag he always carries, big enough to hold his lunch and a bottle of water.'

'Or maybe wine!' another man offered.

'Whatever it was, he sat down beside me on the rock and asked me where I'd learned my trade. He wasn't in any hurry. We talked about the weather and the price of lobsters, and then he asked me about headage on sheep. He seemed in the best of spirits. He said he was going out to catch a pollock for his dinner, and that he'd give me the rest of the catch if I was still there when he got back. I helped him push the boat down the slip. He rowed out past the Carraig and started the outboard. He raised his hand and waved, and that was the last I saw of him.'

'You're sure he had the oars with him?' Woody asked.

'Didn't I see them with my own two eyes!'

'There were no oars in the boat when she was found.'

'You'd think a smart man would carry enough petrol to take him home,' another man put in.

'What did I tell you? Tight as tuppence in a rag.'

'It's a mystery,' the old man said. 'Like hell and original sin, some things can never be explained.'

'Does his wife ever come down here?' Woody asked.

'You mean Spindrift. Now she's a darlin'. She talks to everyone. She never goes out in the boat with him, but she does all her own shopping, and she never has to carry it home. There's always someone to help her, and then she'll ask him in and give him a good big glass of whisky and a plate of home-made biscuits. They say her biscuits are as big as cartwheels.'

'Spindrift is the opposite of Spume,' someone said.

'They're both the same,' the old man explained. 'When the sun is shining, I'd be hard put to tell the difference.'

They turned and watched the ten o'clock news from where they stood. Woody watched Sweetman giving the accepted version of events and then saying as an afterthought that there was a growing swell of local opinion that suspected foul play. People were beginning to ask questions. What happened to the oars? And what happened to Mr Maguire's lunch bag? Where was his hand-line? If he had tried to swim ashore, surely he'd have left his jacket and trousers behind in the boat? Some people were beginning to wonder if there was more to the Taoiseach's disappearance than meets the eye. Woody couldn't help marvelling at Sweetman's ingenuity. Without saying anything of substance, he had planted a seed that he would nurture regularly and diligently for however long the story ran. Sweetman was a cynic who believed in nothing except his own powers of mischievous invention. That was what kept him going—that and the fact that the world was full of people who loved nothing better than a good conspiracy.

'That man on the television knows more than he's letting on,' Fergus said.

'What can he know that we don't?' one of the others asked.

'I'll bet he's been talking to someone local.'

'Josie Hynes, who else? It was Josie who found the boat.'

'Josie's head was always full of nonsense, and nonsense spreads like wildfire,' Fergus summed up.

After four pints of Guinness, Woody slept soundly. The following morning he asked Josie Hynes if he'd take him out for a day's fishing. Josie said he was going out anyway and to come along if he felt like it. Josie was waiting for him on the slip with two fishing rods and two hand-lines. At first, Josie was silent. He did everything that needed to be done without once looking at Woody. They headed into the wind, Josie in the stern and Woody facing him on the middle thwart. When Woody asked him what he thought of Maguire's disappearance, he said quite simply that Maguire had been kidnapped.

'It was on the news last night, but not spelt out. A nod is as good as a wink …' he added.

'Why would anyone want to kidnap Maguire?'

'For a ransom, don't you see? Or maybe it was a splinter group from the North. The world is a dangerous place these days. No one knows what's on anyone's mind.'

They headed straight out into the wider bay. Josie showed him where he'd found Maguire's boat. 'This is the very spot. If you look over my shoulder you'll see the spire of the Protestant church in line with the White House Hotel.'

Of course, there was no telling how far the boat had drifted before being discovered. One thing was certain: a sensible man, even a strong swimmer, wouldn't think of swimming ashore. If Maguire had run out of petrol and lost his oars, he would have been better off staying in the boat in the hope of being found.

'The wind was from the east, blowing off the land,' Josie explained. 'It was a strong wind, strong enough to blow you all the way to America. When I told the schoolmaster that the boat was empty, nothing in her except a bottle of holy water, he said that was how the *Marie Celeste* was found, apart from the holy water.'

'He couldn't have been thirsty,' Woody said. 'If he had been, he'd have drunk the holy water.'

Josie cast a critical eye in his direction. 'Old Fergus said he was carrying a bag. God knows what was in it. But that's another story. Inverrone is swarming with journalists and cameramen, and every man jack of them has his own story. By the time Sunday comes there will be as many stories as journalists. It's the world we live in, and there's no changing it.'

The sky was cloudy. They motored up and down the bay, trailing their hand-lines to no avail. Woody had brought sandwiches and beer, which they shared in silence. Then they went back to the shadow of the land and allowed the boat to drift, while Josie kept complaining about the poor take. Still, by evening they had caught half a dozen pollock and thirteen mackerel between them. Woody was more than happy; he considered it a day well spent. He left his share of the catch with Josie and walked back to the village, thinking that perhaps there might be something in Sweetman's theory after all.

6

Coming out of the greengrocer's, Anna ran into Woody. She had driven down to the cottage that morning, thinking that it might help if she met some of the locals who'd seen or talked to Jim on the fatal afternoon. She had already spoken to the police, but they were no help at all. She simply could not believe that she'd never see her Jim again. Woody was full of sympathy, as you'd expect. He was an old friend, and at times like this friends were precious. He carried her shopping, and, so as not to break a custom, she invited him in for a drink. She wished to talk to someone she knew, and she wanted to hear what Woody had to say, and in particular what he would be saying in his column on Sunday. As an old friend of his, she might even manage to influence his opinion.

'I think Sweetman is barking up the wrong tree,' he said.

'And what tree should he be barking up?' she asked.

'It isn't as simple as he makes out. At this stage no one has all the answers.' It was in his interest to keep his true thoughts from Anna.

'Do you think he drowned?' she pursued.

'Unfortunately, it's a possibility, but only a possibility.'

'Jim is a strong swimmer,' she said. 'At home he swims twice a week.'

'There are strong currents in the bay here. He suffered from arrhythmia. He could have had a heart attack in the water, or he could have got cramp.'

'Unfortunately, the evidence could point in that direction,' she conceded. It was not what she believed, but she thought it wise not to share her true thoughts with a man who was obviously on the lookout for a new slant on a straight story. Deep in her heart she knew that Jim was still alive, and that he'd get in touch with her as soon as the time was ripe. In the weeks before his disappearance, he had been withdrawn and self-absorbed. Quite possibly, he might even have had a threat from the New Invincibles, for whom the Northern Ireland peace talks were anathema. He wouldn't have told her because he knew she was a worrier. Jim was shrewd; he was lying doggo and he would send for her as soon as the coast was clear. In the meantime it was in his interest and in hers to give the impression that he had drowned.

The moment she heard the news on the radio, she went to his study to see if his journal was still in the drawer of his writing desk. It had gone. She knew Jim as well as she knew herself. He was a man of set habits. His journal was important to him. He called it his insurance against a rainy day, and he wrote it up every night before going to bed. She used to make fun of the precious tome, calling it the *Book of Me, Moi and Mé Féin*. Like all men, he had his little rituals. He never took his journal on holiday, but he always took it to the cottage on their weekends away. She had searched every room in the cottage without finding any trace of it. Wherever he had gone, he had taken the hefty volume with him. It was that more than anything else that convinced her he was in hiding.

She invited Woody to stay to dinner because it was in her interest, and Jim's, to have a friendly wolf in the pack. Already the wolves were whimpering. They would howl at their loudest in the Sunday papers.

'Dinner is nothing special,' she explained, 'only cold chicken and salad, but maybe the Volnay will make up for it. Jim always kept a supply of it here.' She did not mention that out of the case he had brought down there were only two bottles left. Wherever he had gone, he wouldn't run dry.

'So what will you be writing for Sunday?' she asked when they had finished the bottle.

'I was planning to weigh up all the possibilities and come down in favour of accidental death by drowning as the most convincing explanation.'

'Do you have to mention the other possibilities? It will only give ammunition to the conspiracy theorists.'

'You needn't worry; I'll make them look ridiculous. The police are right for once. The statement they issued after Sweetman's programme put it in a nutshell: "We have yet to complete our investigations. We are not treating the Taoiseach's disappearance as suspicious at this time." ' He didn't agree with the police, but there were times when a journalist must hang fire in the service of the greater public good. On this occasion it so happened that he would be pleasing Anna as well, which in the long run was not unimportant. To write the definitive biography he would need access to Maguire's papers, and Anna was now the sole custodian of his archive.

He didn't outstay his welcome. When they'd had coffee, he said he felt tired after his day's fishing and that he was planning to have an early night. He'd enjoyed talking to her, but it was sad to observe the depredations of the years in her face. She was no longer the Anna he had loved as a young man. It wasn't just physical deterioration; it was a kind of lignification of the personality that he had often observed in elderly wives who had surrendered their individuality in long service to a self-centred bighead. The Anna in his imagination was the soul of effervescence. She had lost her originality of mind and most of her verbal exuberance. She used to be so unpredictable; you never knew what she'd come out with next. Now she spoke like a suspicious politician confronted with a journalist searching for a chink in her armour. But perhaps her mind was on Jim. Though she'd had a terrible shock, she obviously hadn't lost hope. 'There's expectation from the sea, but not from the land,' she'd said, translating an old Irish proverb. It gave him an insight into her thinking. She was still hoping against hope that he'd be back.

When Woody had gone, she put Mozart's String Quintet in C Major on Jim's CD player and poured herself a glass of Balvenie, her favourite single malt. She'd had very little of the wine at dinner because she needed to keep her wits about her for Jim's sake, especially in the company of a journalist who never missed a trick. She lay back on the sofa and closed her eyes. She had often been alone in the cottage before, but she'd never felt so alone before because Jim was always somewhere in the offing—the word drew her up sharp. Of course, he was still somewhere in the offing, somewhere in the shadows that surrounded her; the only difference was that she didn't know precisely where. She had to admit that over the years they had gradually drifted apart. He never stole up behind her any more to surprise her with an enveloping hug, and he'd stopped lifting her clean off the floor in his arms and whispering nonsense in her ear, but he was scrupulous in his attention to her every need, especially on the rare occasions when she went down with flu.

Unlike most politicians, Jim was a good man. He had presided over the most prosperous period in the history of the State, but, unlike some politicians she knew, he'd refused to avail of the many opportunities that came his way to feather his own nest. In spite of what journalists said, he simply wasn't interested in money; he had put both houses and the cottage in her name because, he joked, she would be highly unlikely to run off with them. Once, when she'd asked him if there was anything in the world he'd like to own, he said, 'Achill for its people. The sea isn't for sale.' In the early years of their marriage they went to Achill every summer, and then he suddenly lost interest. They began going to France instead. Paris, he said, was the most civilised city in the world. He saw London as 'little better than a shoppers' Disneyland', wilting under the weight of a history that was foreign to most of those who roamed its streets.

There was a silly side to Jim; he often did the silliest things just to prove a point. He once walked the length of Oxford Street from Marble Arch to Tottenham Count Road and claimed that he'd heard only eighteen native English speakers on the way. When she asked him who counted as a native English speaker, he laughed at what he called her naïvety. 'In a hundred years' time the lingo spoken on the streets of London will have become incomprehensible to most proper Englishmen.' That was Jim on his high horse, but most of the time he was sensible, and anyhow he wouldn't be Jim without his moments of silliness. Furthermore, she knew that he only indulged his silly side while they were alone together. He'd never say these things to any of his friends, except possibly Bill MacBride who was another old blather with a weakness for foolish fantasies.

Unlike MacBride, Jim was an accomplished actor; the man the nation saw on television and in Dáil debates was not the real Jim at all. On television he looked at ease with himself and at home in the world. He was light-hearted and cheerful, always ready to turn the tables on an interviewer with a joke, even if the joke was on himself. Then he would come home and shut himself up in his study for an hour to lick his wounds. He resented the awful familiarity of journalists, which he found offensive, not to mention their unspoken assumption that he was out to delude the public for his own unworthy ends. He would readily admit to her that as a politician he was merely a salesman of second-hand ideas, that his only gift was his ability to make people listen and be persuaded, but he also said that he would never admit such a thing to anyone else, and that pleased her because it showed that she was the only person he could trust.

To understand Jim, you needed to know about his upbringing. He never knew his mother or father; as a week-old baby he was dumped on the doorstep of a childless TD and his wife, who said that she'd keep the baby because she'd always wanted a fair-haired boy. The baby looked healthy and well cared for. He was wrapped in a white christening shawl and placed in an expensive wicker basket. On his bib was pinned a birthday card on which was inscribed a poem in an italic hand:

> *I am of Ireland*
> *And of the holy land of Ireland.*
> *Cast out by preachy piety,*
> *I beg you in your charity*
> *Bring up my son in Ireland.*

The word 'son' was blotted, as if by the writer's tears. The poem touched the hearts of the childless couple. As they didn't know the baby's name, they gave him their own surname and had him christened James in the hope that he might be great. When he was four, they adopted a three-year-old girl called Sarah to keep him company, but in spite of their best efforts the two children never got on. Sarah was headstrong and demanding while Jim was good-natured and obedient. He was also bright. His foster parents didn't have to spend a penny on his education; he won a scholarship to secondary school, and another scholarship to university. There he never talked about his mysterious origins. To most people he was the son of Mick Maguire, TD for East

Mayo, famous in his time for never having asked a question in the Dáil.

Given his history, perhaps it was no wonder that Jim saw himself as a man on a divinely inspired mission. Like Moses, another basket baby, he would become leader of his people. And like Moses, he would be no ordinary leader. He would climb a mountain above the reach of other politicians, above the grey world of grubby compacts and compromises. He looked around for a modern hero to emulate and found him in General de Gaulle. He could never aspire to de Gaulle's towering stature, but he would emulate his incorruptibility, and perhaps match it.

At first, success came easily. He was elected to his foster father's old seat in parliament, and within ten years he was leader of his party. He became Taoiseach for the first time at the early age of forty-three. He saw politics as a game with its own obscure rules, and for a time he seemed to enjoy its verbal battles, its uncertainties, and its occasional inspirational victories. The only raincloud in his heavens was his foster-sister, Sarah, who had become dependent on a daily bottle of vodka to keep her happy and relied on Jim's generosity to provide it. She kept pestering him for money, and he kept reasoning with her to no avail. When she began talking to gossip columnists about his past, he saw it as the last straw. He refused to see her any more, and that, of course, ignited more tinder. He was no longer a leader whom no one cared to question. Soon he was a mortal man whose dubious origins were common knowledge, and unfortunately they were origins that invited both reductive speculation and psychological probing.

The gossip that resulted wounded him in a place where no dart had reached before. She had tried to make him see its irrelevance, telling him that no one took these things seriously, but nothing she said could salve his terrible loss of pride. For the first time in their life together, she realised how vulnerable he was. He rarely watched television with her; he spent more and more time alone in his study. He had withdrawn from a world of which he had once been king.

She couldn't say precisely when he had lost his original vision of himself. Perhaps it was around the time of his fifty-fourth birthday. She had bought him the latest biography of de Gaulle as a present, and she had booked a table at his favourite restaurant, but he said that as it was his birthday he was going to cook her dinner at home.

'We'll have a mixed grill,' he said. 'I'll cook lamb cutlets, gammon steak, black pudding, sausages and tomatoes. You fry the eggs. I can never manage a decent egg.'

She thought it strange at the time, but she said nothing. As it turned out, it was quite a good dinner. The cooking was passable, and he was attentive and amusing, as if it were her birthday, not his. She reasoned that he'd had a difficult day and that quite simply he'd been exposed to too many people and wished for nothing more than a quiet evening at home with his wife.

They must have sat at the table for an hour just talking about this and that. Then he said, out of the blue, 'No one gets through a life in politics without having to make one or two pacts with the Devil.' At first she paid no attention, thinking that it was Jim being overscrupulous, but when he proposed a toast to Faust, she asked him what he meant.

'Faust was a serious man. I admire serious men, they are so rare.'

'Surely you wouldn't want to be Faust?'

'I'd like to have devoted my life to the pursuit of knowledge.'

'But think of all the good you've done the people of this country.'

'Politics is a second-rate activity. As Enoch Powell said, "All political careers end in failure."'

'To Faust, then,' she said, and raised her glass with a smile.

She attached no importance to the toast at the time. Now, for Jim's sake, she herself would have to make compromises and compacts. Neither Kevin Woody nor Tony Sweetman could be described as the Devil, but she would have to keep in with them because that is what Jim would expect of her.

7

Having filed his piece on Maguire's disappearance, Woody drove back to Dublin on Saturday afternoon. He was glad to be getting home because the capital was where he wished to be. It was the centre of his personal universe and the place where he felt most at ease. The country might be fine for poets and tourists, but it was no place for a man who valued his comforts and liked to have them within easy reach. He got up early on Sunday morning and, without waiting to shave, went out to buy the papers as was his custom. This was no ordinary Sunday: today he had a personal stake in the news and in how the story was seen to be unfolding. He was playing two games at once, and it was no part of his intention to win one at the expense of the other—both were equally important.

First, he cast an eye over the headlines and lead paragraphs to get the general drift of things. The known facts were common to all; what differed was the interpretation and the degree of speculation considered acceptable. His own piece was the most level-headed of the bunch. He was pleased to see that he had anticipated every tom-fool argument, that he had weighed every conceivable theory in the balance and given his verdict. His stance might not satisfy everyone, but it would satisfy readers with both feet on the ground.

Jane arrived at eleven-thirty, hotfoot from ten o'clock in the Pro-Cathedral. He himself had given up the soother after his mother's funeral, but Jane, bless her, was still a staunch upholder of the old traditions. There were many things about her that he admired, and the greatest of these was her unshakeable knowledge of her own mind. Compared with her, he himself was a weathercock, content to face into every wind that blew. That wasn't completely true, of course, but that was how she saw it. She accused him of fence-sitting, of not knowing the difference between right and wrong, and of not caring much about anybody or anything. On one occasion she had called him 'a hard-hearted bastard'. Still, she was as necessary to him as his daily four pints of Guinness. She had made herself an indispensable component of his life. She might be a source of occasional aggro, but where would he be without her? She was the yeast that caused his daily bread to rise.

'You're a disgrace to humankind,' she said. 'You've been up since dawn and you still smell like a ferret.'

'I left the sirloin on the worktop,' he said. 'I'll leave you to it while I shower and shave.'

He had deliberately postponed his ablutions until after her arrival because he knew that she liked to be left to her own devices in the kitchen. 'Your kitchen is too small for two, especially two who don't see eye to eye,' she would say. Now he never crossed swords with her on culinary matters. Once, when he did, she appointed him cook for the day, an honorary office he had no wish to occupy again.

When he had made himself sweet-smelling, he poured her a stiff gin and tonic and a stiffer one for himself. She had already put the sirloin in the oven, peeled the potatoes, parsnips and carrots, and shelled the peas. She was nothing if not efficient. He thanked his lucky stars that she wasn't his editor.

'You can kiss me now,' she said, 'with all the perfumes of Arabia playing about your ears.'

'I knew my aftershave would get you going.'

'You know nothing about modern women, you big troglodyte.'

He led her into the living room and told her that he'd like her opinion on how the Maguire story was playing. They both went through the papers while he made an occasional mental note of new angles that no one else had thought of. That was the interesting thing about the news: even the most inane article could suggest yet another unexplored angle. Within half an hour he had assembled enough new ideas to justify another article. In one sense he lived hand to mouth, and in another he lived on his fertile imagination. What the reading public didn't know was that journalists dined off each other: even the lowliest practitioner of the craft often, quite unwittingly, gave another journalist the germ for a tour de force.

'It's all speculation,' she said. 'No one knows the truth, and no one ever will.'

'I avoided speculation in my piece. I confined myself to the known facts.'

'Who wants facts on a Sunday? Facts are for weekdays. On Sunday people want something to wallow in. You leave nothing to the imagination, Woody. Your article may be true, but it's flat—it didn't make me wonder. We all want to believe in something *beyond* the facts. If you went to Mass on a Sunday, you'd know what I'm talking about.'

In the reference to religion he smelt trouble. He had learnt to distinguish between Jane being serious and Jane winding him up.

'I fancy another gin and tonic,' he said.

'Isn't that you to a tee? You can never discuss anything sensibly. At the first hint of seriousness you make for the nearest exit. As it happens, I'll have another gin with more tonic than last time.'

He came and sat beside her on the sofa. 'We'll go to bed,' he said. 'You know how opposition gets me going. I just can't wait any longer.'

'And what about the roast?'

'We have a good half-hour. Just enough time for a quickie.'

'A quickie! Isn't that what you'd like!? Well, you're not getting it. Why? Because I've been here before. Because I didn't come down in the last shower.'

'But I haven't seen you for a whole week. You have no idea of the remorseless urgency of my need.'

'Remorseless! I like it! Then get it over with! But we'll have to go to bed properly after lunch.'

He couldn't help admiring her. Her Sunday lunch was the best meal of the week. Try as he might, he could never come up with her roast potatoes and parsnips, and her Yorkshire pudding was light and airy, threatening to float up off the plate.

'Tell me what you did in Conamara,' she said, as they sat down to lunch.

'I went fishing with the man who found Maguire's boat adrift, and I caught more pollock in four hours than he did.'

'Never mind the catch, what did you learn?'

'Two things: either Maguire drowned swimming to land or he had the help of another man in another boat.'

'So you think it possible that he's still alive?'

'It's possible, but highly unlikely.'

'Then why didn't you say so in your article?'

'Because it isn't what I believe.'

'It didn't take you three days to come to that conclusion. What else did you do?'

'I got the locals to fill me in on the background.'

'And what did you learn?'

'They had a nickname for Maguire. They called him Spume, and his wife Spindrift.'

'"Spindrift!" One of the papers has a picture of her. I suppose you interviewed her as well.'

'I met her briefly.'

'What age is she?

'I would put her in her early fifties.'

'Is she good-looking?'

'She may have been good-looking, but that was a long time ago.'

'And what does she think?'

'She's convinced against the odds that Maguire is still alive, that he's in hiding from the New Invincibles.'

'So it's in her interest to pretend that he's dead and put the terrorists off the scent?'

'I suppose you could put it like that.'

'And isn't that what you believe as well?'

'I have no axe to grind; I'm just reporting on what I see before me.'

'Now I know where you stand. She told you what to say, and you flowered it up to make it look good.'

'I'm no one's cat's paw. I stand by every word in my article.'

'Come on, Woody, you could write an article from any one of a dozen points of view. Isn't that what journalism is about? Well, I believe that Maguire was up to his neck in shady business deals. He wasn't what he pretended to be. Will you write about that in your next "think-piece"?'

'You know I can't make up the news. What I write must have a basis in fact.'

'So what's the difference between Spindrift and me?'

'I don't know what you mean.'

'You're willing to write what she thinks, but you're not willing to do the same for me. I know what you're up to, me bucko. I'm not as stupid as you think.'

'What am I up to?'

'She's a well-off widow. You want to get into her big roomy drawers before someone else does.'

'Jane! How can you think such a thing?'

'Then write an article giving my opinion. Otherwise, no sex for afters.'

He knew that argument was futile.

'I'll see what I can do. You write the article, and I'll translate it into journalese,' he said, fervently hoping that she wouldn't put him to the test.

8

They went to bed immediately after lunch, and they stayed in bed until seven, snoozing between bouts of lovemaking. When he'd had as much as he could take, he told her that he was dying for a black coffee stiffened with a shot of Jameson.

'You're never happy, are you? You've had enough sex to keep you quiet for another week, and now you want something else, you big baby.'

'We'll wash up together while the coffee percolates. Life is full of surprises. Who knows what's next on the agenda?'

'I do, and it's not more of the same.'

At eight, she said she must be off. As he kissed her at the door, she put her hand on his crotch and squeezed it. 'Dead as the woolly mammoth. But don't worry, I'll resurrect him for you again next Sunday.'

Pleased to have the house to himself again, he was about to settle down to a quiet evening of television when Anna phoned.

'Oh, hello, Anna,' he cooed in the hope of concealing his irritation.

'You've seen the papers!' she said. 'Aren't they awful? Not a word of the truth. Nothing but scandal and chicanery. Your article was the only sensible one among them.'

'All I did was to tell it as I see it.'

'Sweetman is a shit. He was never done sucking up to Jim. At last he's come out in his true colours.'

'His piece is way over the top. No one will believe a word of it.'

'I'm back in Howth. I'm hoping you can come round to lunch tomorrow. It won't be anything special, just the two of us. I'd like to have your opinion on what we should do next.'

He told her that he had a meeting at ten, and that he'd be with her no later than twelve-thirty. The meeting was a white lie, but he thought it advisable to give the impression that he was up to his neck in work. Since Maguire never seemed to have a minute to spare, she probably judged all men by how busy they appeared to be. She wasn't being open with him, of course. There was something on her mind that she hadn't put into words. 'I'd just like *your* opinion on what *we* should do next.' What could she have meant? He would tread carefully until the way ahead became clear. For a split second he wondered if perhaps he might be out of his depth.

***

She put down the phone and stood looking at it, as if expecting it to ring. There weren't many people she could turn to—most of Jim's friends weren't hers. Although Woody was a journalist, she felt at ease with him. He seemed straightforward, and he had once been fond of her. She'd felt sorry for him at the time because there was never any question of her falling in love with him, which was something he'd found difficult to accept.

She had seen him then as rather gauche, less sophisticated than Jim. Now a point in his favour was his lack of style. Unlike Sweetman, he always looked dishevelled and somehow unready. No one would ever call him a smoothie. Was it possible that the rough exterior concealed a sentimental heart?

Since they last met, she had made a disturbing discovery. Stored in a cardboard box in a corner of the study was Jim's journal, all six volumes. She had assumed that he'd taken the missing journal with him, which had led her to believe that he might have absconded. His journal was his insurance against an impecunious old age. Surely he wouldn't have absconded without it? Now she did not know what to think. A terrible thought occurred to her: she might never see her Jim again. She did not know if she should mention the journal to Woody. As she had expected, he was late for lunch. He arrived panting and perspiring, as if he had pedalled hard all the way.

'I hope I haven't ruined lunch,' he apologised.

'We're having a cold lunch. I knew you'd be late. Journalists, like politicians, are never on time.'

'I've been thinking,' she said when they'd sat down, 'that someone needs to write a considered reply to all this wild speculation, if only to restore the balance in favour of common sense, and it seems to me that you are the man best qualified to do it.'

'I had been thinking along the same lines, though I must admit that readers find more excitement in conspiracy theories than in boring old common sense. Just think of the amount of ink spilt over the deaths of President Kennedy and Princess Diana. The appeal to reason will never prevail over the desire to read about skulduggery in high places.'

'In this instance it isn't so much skulduggery as mystery. If Jim had had a heart attack and died at home in bed, none of this would have happened. It's only because of the uncertainty surrounding his disappearance that we're having this conversation. Disappearance or death? Which is it? Even I can't be altogether sure.'

'Nothing will end the speculation except an inquest, which could be months away.'

'In the meantime we can only do our best. I'll give you all the help I can. I think Bill MacBride might be the right man to start with. He was Jim's best friend. I say that though I never liked Bill myself. A gossiping old windbag, I always thought.'

Woody was good company. She enjoyed talking to him. She could see that he wasn't well off. The cuffs of his shirt were frayed, his shoes scuffed and unpolished. But perhaps he was slovenly by nature. Besides, men who lived alone often failed to look after themselves. Still, there must have been women in his life. He'd look passable if only he'd shave off his sideburns and spruce himself up a bit. It was the sort of thing she couldn't tell him, the sort of thing that only a wife or girlfriend could say.

He was obviously an admirer of Jim. He had told her that Jim's achievement would not be appreciated for many years to come. 'When something is done well, everyone thinks it's easy,' he explained. 'Everyone begins to think that they themselves could do it. It's only when someone else takes over that the unwelcome truth becomes apparent.' He was right, of course. Jim was gone less than a fortnight, and already the coalition was falling apart. Her personal mission was now to protect Jim's reputation and to ensure the survival of his political legacy. Already she could see that some of his ex-colleagues, in jockeying for the party leadership, were trying to blame him for their own mistakes. Unfortunately, she was not a political animal. She was relying on Woody's help in what she was seeking to achieve. She would have to do some serious thinking before their next meeting. It was by no means clear to her how much she should tell him. She even wondered if in talking to him she was being unfaithful to Jim's memory. Jim never talked to journalists off the cuff: though well able to think on his feet, he took the precaution of thinking everything out in advance, and that was what she herself must do.

Jim was master of the art of the possible. He had led four coalition governments, holding together parties that were by instinct at sixes and sevens. In the common view he was the most adroit politician of his generation. If he had been running a country that mattered on the international stage, he would have been seen as a statesman with the courage and vision that go with a deep sense of history. For a grand exemplar, he did not turn to Whitehall or Washington. From one of his many trips to Paris, he brought back a book of de Gaulle's maxims, which he kept on his desk as a kind of aide-memoire. Like the General, he believed that a successful politician cannot always share his innermost thoughts with the public. When she asked him if a successful politician could be an honest man, he smiled and said that it was not the kind of question a successful politician would ask himself. When she questioned him further, he said that if de Valera had had half of de Gaulle's gifts as a politician and statesman there would have been no civil war and no partition of Ireland. Of course, there was a less than serious side to Jim. She suspected that he admired de Gaulle in particular for his summary dismissal of Harold Macmillan. The Olympian General didn't deign to argue with the unflappable Old Etonian; he simply said *"Non!"* and slammed the Common Market door shut in his face. 'What else could he have done?' Jim used to ask. 'How else can you deal with a man who is paralysed by a sense of his own superior history?' In spite of that, Jim used to make fun of de Gaulle. At parties he was fond of mimicking de Gaulle's French; he used to say that no one had heard real French spoken who had not heard de Gaulle.

Of course, he never said any of these things on public platforms—they were said to his friends, or to her over dinner. Whether he believed them himself was another matter. He was fond of saying that the Irish are an amoral people, more superstitious than religious, entirely lacking in any sense of civic ethics. 'They love the rogue,' he would smile, 'the cute hoor and the conman who thrives at the expense of the highly respectable and those who look down on their neighbours. Your typical Irishman is an anarchist without knowing it. And that is why there will never be a boring, suburban middle class in Ireland. How can anyone govern a country of seditious poets who spout poetry in the shop and the pub, and won't take the trouble to write it?'

That was Jim in after-dinner mode, surrounded by friends he could trust. But there was another Jim, the gloom-laden Jim who sometimes came home and went straight to his study. She could imagine the routine. He would pour himself a whisky or two and slump into his armchair while dinner shrivelled in the oven. There was no point in calling him. Finally, he would emerge and they would both sit down in silence, daring each other to be the first to speak. She dreaded those evenings, but fortunately they were rare. She often wondered about the cause. Was it something in his nature, or was it just that he'd had a very bad day? In spite of appearances, he was a sensitive spirit, which is why he used to say that in politics you need the hide of an elephant. He once seemed on the point of giving her an inkling of his thoughts. 'I'm not cut out for politics,' he said. 'The price is too high and the pay too low.'

'You're not doing too badly,' she smiled encouragingly.

'I should have been an artist, a poet perhaps. I read a poem by Edward Thomas after I came in this evening, and as I read it I recalled that something similar had happened to me. Then I read another poem by his friend Robert Frost, and knew that I, too, had had an echo of Frost's experience.'

'And what are those two magical poems?' she asked jokingly. 'I'd like to read them to see if they resonate with me as well.'

He went to his study and came back with two books. He read her 'The Other' and 'After Apple-Picking'. Then he said that they wouldn't talk further about the poems in case they might puncture the balloon. 'Poetry, like religion, is a private thing,' he explained. 'The more you talk about it, the more you flatten it. There must be a special circle in hell for theologians and literary critics.' This morning, as she read 'After Apple-Picking' again, three lines hit her square in the face:

> *For I have had too much*
> *Of apple-picking: I am overtired*
> *Of the great harvest I myself desired.*

Then she read 'The Other', and paused over the last three lines:

> *He goes: I follow: no release*
> *Until he ceases. Then I also shall cease.*

The question a journalist had asked her at the weekend returned to form a stricture in her chest. 'Was your husband depressed, Mrs Maguire?' Another journalist had asked her if Mr Maguire had ever talked of suicide. Yet another asked if, like John F. Kennedy, he was oversexed. There was no end to their insensitivity. What made their questions so unbearable was the thought that there might be a legitimate reason for all of them. Jim wasn't depressed, as far as she could tell, but he was hard pressed. The economy was running out of steam, the smaller parties in the coalition had grown restive, and Jim was tired of going cap in hand to what he called 'a bunch of excitable pygmies'. Did he talk of suicide? No, he didn't, but he had talked about getting away from it all one day. Was he oversexed? Unlike Kennedy, he didn't get headaches from having to go without, at least as far as she could tell, but beyond doubt he was sexually demanding, more demanding in their early days than she cared to recall. In the last few years he had troubled her hardly at all. She suspected that he had a mistress or two. Once, when he was very late home, she took his coat and kissed his cheek. 'You stink of unsubtle perfume,' she smiled, though she didn't feel like smiling.

'Then you must buy me an aftershave that doesn't offend you.' She could see that he was deeply offended. She had caught him out. Worse, she had reduced him in his own eyes, an unforgivable offence. After that he never troubled her for sex any more.

She wouldn't tell any of that to Woody, but she would have to make some concessions for the sake of appearances. She could give him the odd hint to keep him happy, but she would keep her distance in case he got any ideas. As he was unmarried, he might harbour an ambition to slip into Jim's shoes, impossible though that was for her to contemplate. Still, she would have to keep him on her side for Jim's sake. He would never do the dirty on Jim while she remained his friend. She would not be obvious. She would leave the door open, as if in a fit of absent-mindedness. As Jim once put it, 'There is no need to encourage journalists; they're a dab hand at encouraging themselves.'

9

Woody arrived in Neary's just before twelve to find Sweetman already halfway down his pint.

'I got here early so as to grab the window table. I hate being surrounded by gossiping shoppers.'

'I sympathise entirely. As journalists, we must turn a deaf ear to all gossip!'

'Now don't be silly, Woody. There's gossip and gossip. In the right hands it can become literature.'

'Literature is about the truth. I didn't detect much of that in last Sunday's papers.'

'Politics isn't about the truth, so how can truth come into the reporting of politics?'

'If it isn't about the truth, then what is it about?'

'Simply, what can be made to look like the truth. Verisimilitude as opposed to verity. You and I are just thimble-riggers. We deal in illusion and the kind of legerdemain that encourages a momentary suspension of disbelief.'

'Sometimes you talk more shit than sense,' Woody said.

'We must take comfort where we can. We're both among the best illusionists in town.'

'I have no fancy theories. I just write what I see before me.'

'This is the story of a lifetime, my dear Woody. It will run and run. Why? Because it has a beginning, a middle, and no known ending. Every man jack of us is free to make up his own ending, and every time you change the ending you cast new light on what has gone before. We've got people talking. Everyone in every pub up and down the country has his own theory, all of them plausible but equally unreliable. We've created a loose baggy monster that none of us can control. It's a journalist's feast, I tell you. Don't deny yourself a share of the nosh.'

'I thought your piece sublimely imaginative,' Woody said.

'That was just a sprat. Wait till you see the mackerel!'

'So there's more to come?'

'As a journalist and fisherman, you know what I mean. I've had several bites already.'

'I'll look forward to next Sunday, then.'

'Tell me, Woody. Have you really been nobbled?'

'I don't know what you're getting at.'

'Nobbled by the widow. She tried to nobble me, but I pretended not to understand. There are times in the life of any journalist when it pays to play stupid.'

'I'm not in anyone's pocket. I knew Maguire better than most. I have a fair idea of what was within his capacity and what was not.'

'So you reckon all this speculation is so much hogwash?'

'It isn't the truth.'

'Look at what's happened. We've invented a life story that no one had dreamt of before. Better still, we've inspired people to think for themselves.'

'I refuse to argue. Let's talk about something else.'

'Let's talk about the widow. How to describe a woman who writes fairy stories for children and doesn't believe in them herself? Is she a hypocrite, pure and simple, or a journalist in disguise?'

'She's made a name for herself. She's good at what she does.'

'So are we. Now what's her game, would you say? I bet you haven't worked that one out.'

'Like any wife, she's concerned about the scandalous things that are being written about her husband.'

'So she thinks Maguire is still alive, does she?'

'I wouldn't know. To me it seems unlikely.'

'It's still a good story, capable of development, so let's reduce it to its essentials. A man of some importance vanishes at sea, which gives rise to a host of unanswerable questions. Did he drown? If so, was it an accident or suicide? If it was suicide, was he depressed? Or perhaps he did a bunk with the help of a third party? If so, what was he trying to escape from? Is there a scandal brewing, and if so, is it sexual or financial? If it's sexual, what kind of sex is involved and with whom? If it's financial, who else had his or her hand in the national till? As you can see, the questions are endless. As journalists with a nose for the truth, it's in our interest to keep the story alive until the final truth is made known.'

'The final truth may never be known.'

'And isn't that what makes for interest? As a topic, it's inexhaustible. So why don't we share our thoughts? I'll tell you my thoughts if you tell me yours.'

'Or to put it another way, I'll show you mine if you show me yours.'

'That's what I like about you, Woody, the way you reduce everything to the sexual essentials. So let me go first. Be assured, I haven't forgotten my elusive courtesan. I never give up the chase; I'm still on her tail. She's somewhere in Paris, and I've got a friendly *journaliste politique* on the case.'

'But that has nothing to do with Maguire's disappearance.'

'*Au contraire*, Maguire is probably enjoying her professional favours in a luxurious boudoir somewhere in gay Par-ee. He's a rich man, remember. He can well afford to keep her in style.

I've looked into his financial dealings. I bet there's more money in his Swiss bank accounts than has come from his ministerial salary.'

'Again, speculation.'

'No, not speculation: careful observation. He owns two houses, not to mention a cottage in Conamara and a yacht in Howth harbour. Where on earth did all that money come from? Not from his salary. From immoral earnings perhaps? Or did he have a grubby hand in someone else's greasy till?'

'The speculation gets wilder. There's not a shred of evidence to base a story on.'

'You're very wrong, Woody. Like the widow, I'm convinced Maguire is still alive and enjoying his new-found freedom from us narrow-minded Irish. He'd reached his peak. He was already on the slippery slope. Maguire was a proud man, the type of man who is inclined to exit before he is pushed. Now he is somewhere in Paris, and I shall be knocking on his door when he least expects me.'

'I think you should give up journalism and take to novel writing. With your inflamed imagination, you could write a bestseller.'

'Well, what are your thoughts? I've shown you mine, now show me yours.'

'Let me buy you another pint first. You may need it.'

As he went to the bar to order, Woody had no idea what he should tell Sweetman, whose story was too bizarre for words. More than likely, Sweetman himself did not believe a word of it. It was all a ruse to get him to show his hand. He was nobody's fool. He would repay Sweetman in his own coin. As he ordered, he racked his brains for an equally bizarre version of events. Two young men standing next to him were talking about a third man called McBriney. As he listened to their mysterious exchanges he was reminded of Maguire's best friend, MacBride. It was a gift from heaven. Already a story, every bit as unlikely as Sweetman's, floated unbidden into his mind.

'I'm all ears. Let's have it.' Sweetman raised his glass.

'I've come to the conclusion that the man who holds the key to all this is Bill MacBride. He was Maguire's best friend, the man he talked to every day and met several times a week. The psychological traffic wasn't all one-way; it was a symbiotic relationship. There are those who think that their interest in each other was sexual, but I'm not one of them. I believe that Maguire, like MacBride, was strictly hetero. Their relationship hung entirely on their interest in Parisian courtesans and the services they are happy to provide.'

'So what are you trying to tell me?'

'Like you, I'm convinced that Maguire is still alive, not here but somewhere warmer and less puritanical. I'm also convinced that MacBride will soon be joining him in his pleasure dome. Where it is I don't know, but I suspect it isn't necessarily Paris.'

'So why haven't you come out with any of this in print?'

'I'm still assembling the evidence. When I get it all together, you'll read about it one Sunday and marvel at my nose for the truth.'

'Interesting. So MacBride will be the next man to disappear, you reckon?'

'It's all too possible.'

'You could be on to something. I'll put a tail on MacBride.'

Several times over the following week, thoughts of MacBride floated in and out of Woody's mind. Anna had said that he would be a good man to talk to, and Anna probably knew what she was about. He had interviewed MacBride on business matters once or twice, and had found him full of stories and gossip. He thought in anecdotes rather than in management gobbledegook. As he was dedicated to the practice of lunching well, Woody reckoned that he would be at his most expansive in mid afternoon.

MacBride said he'd meet him in his office at three-thirty, but four o'clock came and he still hadn't turned up. His secretary said that ever since the death of Maguire, 'the boss', as she called him, had not been his usual jaunty self. It was almost four-thirty when MacBride, red-faced and flustered, finally made an appearance.

'Sorry to keep you waiting,' he said when he'd finally settled himself behind his desk. 'I was trying to shake off my tail. Believe it or not, someone is shadowing me, so I instructed my driver to go the long way round and lay a few false trails.'

'Surely it can't be the police?'

'I've had to stop making private phone calls. I know they're listening in. They've squeezed the Maguire saga dry. Now they want to pin something on muggins.'

'If the press is behind it, it's news to me.'

'Not the press as such. It's Sweetman. Jim used to call him the Old Man of the Sea. Try as he might, he couldn't get him off his back.'

'Anna Maguire has been badgering me to write a piece putting all this wild speculation in its place, and I thought you'd be a good man to talk to, since you knew Maguire better than any of us.'

'I knew him and I didn't know him. Jim was a very private man, and a bit of a tease as well. Quite possibly, what he thought and what he said were two different things. He used to say that when a politician is in the trough of the wave, he should be seen to be on the crest. He meant that politics is not about ideas but appearances—in other words, creating the illusion that you are what you are not. The idea was typical Jim, the supreme political tactician, contemptuous of his own sleight of hand.'

MacBride went to his drinks cabinet, and without asking Woody what he'd like, poured two generous Paddy whiskeys. He was in a mood to hold forth, but the more he spoke the less sense he made. Gone were the amusing anecdotes; instead, he was intent on bending Woody's ear about the iniquities of the media. Woody regretted not having met him at nine o'clock in the morning, but still he kept plying him with questions in the hope that he might let something slip.

'You think he's still alive?'

'Jim's involvement in the Northern Ireland peace negotiations made him some very unsavoury enemies. He'd had so much hate mail that he stopped reading it. If Jim is still alive, he's the prisoner of the New Invincibles. But more than likely he has already gone the way of Shergar, another national hero.' There was a catch in his voice as he held up his glass.

'That's not what Anna thinks.'

'I've talked to Anna. Like all women, she's a sentimentalist. Jim was hard-working and hard-headed. He used to say that if you took a dim view of everyone you met, you'd never put a foot wrong. He was half-expecting the fate that overtook him.'

'Isn't it possible that he just got weary of the game and did a bolt? There are rumours that he's somewhere on the continent.'

'There are even rumours that he's gone to Tahiti. He was obsessed with French art. One of his favourite artists was Gauguin.'

'But you don't believe he's in Tahiti?'

'I don't believe in fairy tales. Jim and I were friends. I miss him terribly.' He drew a handkerchief from his pocket and blew his nose. 'I would go into the jungle with Jim knowing that if he came out alive, so would I.'

He spent an hour and a half with MacBride without learning anything except that he was rattled. Either he was laying a false trail or he had some very weighty problems on his mind. He had lost the businessman's urge to dictate the terms of trade.

10

MacBride felt uneasy. The last thing he needed was a pack of inquisitive journalists on his heels, yet here he was at the very centre of the Maguire saga. As he was having a quiet drink with his old friend Maloney in the Shelbourne yesterday afternoon, a young man and a girl came and sat at the next table. They didn't say a word to each other. Instead they began cuddling like overexcited teenagers, while all the time they were listening to what he and Maloney were talking about. He tipped Maloney the wink and they both went to the gents together. The young man soon followed. Rather young to be a policeman, he was obviously one of Sweetman's cub reporters, still too wet behind the ears to make himself inconspicuous. As the three of them stood at the urinals, Maloney began praising Sweetman, saying what a clever journalist he was and how he seemed to know what was going to happen before it had time to happen. The young man took a hint. He shook himself dry and left.

That was only one instance among several. These days he was constantly aware of being shadowed, which wasn't good for his state of mind. He had begun to suspect journalists he'd never suspected before, including Kevin Woody, one of the few hacks Maguire trusted. It was all becoming too much to bear. Jim, being Jim, would have taken it in his stride, of course. He had a fine contempt for his less gifted compatriots, and as he used to say, there were a lot of them about. For Jim's sake and his own, he would have to keep his cool. He would wait patiently till he'd heard from him. Meanwhile, he would have to be careful not to say anything or do anything that might give the game away. Talking to Woody the other day had made him realise how careful he needed to be. He would never again talk to a journalist in the afternoon. He would make the mornings his time for interviews, when he was still fresh and his mind alert to the unspoken question lurking beneath the question asked.

Jim had messed things up. He had given no hint of his intentions. If he were bent on doing a bunk, he should have left no loose ends, no room for conspiracy theories. The missing oars ruined everything. What could he have been thinking of? Surely he should have known that every hack in town would want to know where they'd gone. The missing oars opened the floodgates. Hacks who knew nothing about winds and tides felt obliged to come up with an even more outlandish theory than any of their colleagues. Now that they had exhausted their stock of theories, they had turned the spotlight on Maguire's best friend. In a way he should feel flattered, but nothing in his life had prepared him for the circus that now surrounded him. For the first time he had an insight into the kind of life that Jim must have led and the reasons for the dyke he had built round himself. Jim was engaged in a constant battle to keep his defences in good order and stem the relentless flow of a tide that never turned to ebb. No wonder there were times when he had the impression that he wasn't listening, that he was fighting his inner demons, battling against himself.

What the gentlemen of the press couldn't understand was what Jim had in common with a rather ordinary and unglamorous businessman. Surely, they reasoned, there must be more to their relationship than meets the eye. It was all too typical of the cynicism at the heart of modern journalism. Jim and he had been friends for twenty years or more. If he wanted to buy a plot of land for building development, he would ask Jim whether he thought it a sound idea. More often than not he'd say yes, but now and again he'd say, 'No, it looks more trouble than it's worth.' Similarly, he helped Jim out whenever he could. Jim's government salary was too modest to meet all his expenses, and he appreciated having a friend who could make up the difference between what he earned and what he spent. He was too scrupulous to ask for a loan, but he wouldn't say no to an occasional present. Neither of them kept accounts because they were not bean counters. As friends, they felt there was no need.

They had a joint account in a Swiss bank into which each of them made payments and on which either of them could draw while abroad on business or for pleasure. If he paid in more than Jim, that was only to be expected; and if Jim drew more heavily on their account, that was only because his way of life involved him in unpredictable outlay. This arrangement had seemed eminently reasonable to both of them at the time, but in the present atmosphere of small-minded nitpicking it was in danger of being misinterpreted. Journalists had no concept of the nobility of long friendship. They judged everyone by their own debased standards. Some of them stooped low enough to suggest that he and Jim enjoyed the favours of the same woman at the same time. It was all quite disgusting—so disgusting that he had taken legal advice—but that was only at the prompting of his horrified wife. Maggie, God bless her, had no understanding of the modern world. She was inclined to believe everything she read, and she thought everyone else believed it as well. When he told her that newspapers were there to provide light entertainment, she accused him of being as irresponsible as the journalists who were out to vilify him.

Jim had his own views. 'The bloodhounds are baying,' he said the last time they met. 'Ireland has changed. The civilised reticence of Dev's time is ancient history now. We have a new generation of scribblers whose fathers never handled a shovel. They're all the offspring of accountants and businessmen, and they write like accountants and businessmen. Dev was lucky, living as he did in the age of Frank O'Connor and Seán Ó Faoláin. Those men had their feet on the sod as opposed to the pavement, and they had their heads in the clouds, as literary men should. Today's scribes, with their highfalutin jargon, lack the literary grace of their predecessors.'

That's what he missed most, the way Jim would let himself go in his company and say things he wouldn't have said to anyone else. There was no one to replace him. All he could do now was to wait patiently for the word. He was bound to be in touch once he could see a clear coast ahead. He'd been keeping an eye on their joint account ever since he went missing. No withdrawals had been made in his name. In one sense that was worrying, and in another it was reassuring. Jim was nothing if not scrupulous—a straight shooter and a stickler for straight dealing. Without him, life was empty, all the excitement and tension gone.

He felt so restless in the house at weekends that he started going for long walks on his own. Now and again he went to the local to pass the time. He liked to read the paper over a pint and place a bet whenever he spotted something he fancied. He and Maguire used to talk about the lives they'd lead in retirement. Maguire used to say that he'd spend the time reading and writing. He would laugh at him for saying he'd spend the mornings in the local and the afternoons asleep. Even his local had now lost its magic; more often than not there was no one to talk to, except a few old codgers who never had anything to say. If Jim knew the state he was in, he wouldn't keep him waiting. He'd get in touch straight away.

There was a raffish side to Jim, which became apparent only in Paris. He knew the French of the marketplace as well as the French of the salons. He was not only fluent but quick-witted; he could make the Froggies laugh at jokes in their own language. He knew the back streets of Paris like the back of his hand. They always walked off their dinner, and often he himself would have no idea where they were heading. One evening they ended up in a smoky basement with a jazz band, what Jim called a clip joint, and he could only describe as a knocking shop. Two hostesses brought them their drinks and sat in their laps, burrowing into their groins with their bottoms. Though probably still in their twenties, they were beginning to look raddled. Other hostesses were leading customers through a door with a red curtain at the end of the bar. The heat was overpowering. He couldn't imagine what had got into Jim. It was not his kind of entertainment. Suddenly, Jim looked at his watch. He whispered something in the hostess's ear and she whispered something in her companion's ear. They both laughed and went to the bar.

'We'll be off now,' Jim said. 'Clip joints never change.'

Once outside, they walked briskly.

'What did you make of that?' Jim asked when they'd turned the corner.

'It took me back thirty years. Cheap perfume mixed with cigarette smoke smells the same everywhere. All that was different was the lingo.'

'In Europe there's no longer anything new under the moon. Gauguin had to go all the way to Tahiti, and that was a hundred years ago. If you've got any ideas, let me know.'

He'd thought nothing of the comment at the time, but he now began wondering if Jim had had an idea that he'd kept to himself. Perhaps he wasn't in Paris. Perhaps he wasn't even in Europe. He was a man who delighted in the exotic. He went through a period when he was passionate about the paintings of Henri Rousseau, rhapsodising over what he called the dark ambiguities of *The*

Snake Charmer. Maybe he should phone Anna. She might say something unbeknown to herself that would give him an insight into Jim's thinking as he left for Conamara on that fatal weekend.

'What did you expect?' Anna asked when he said he'd had no word from Jim.

'I don't think he's dead, and if he's still alive, he may be in need of help.'

'Well, there's very little I can do since I don't know where he is. I could put an ad in the paper, I suppose!'

She was refusing to take him seriously. She had always resented his relationship with her husband. Once, when he rang Jim at home, she answered the phone. 'Jim,' she'd called in a put-on mummy voice, 'your friend wants to know if you'll come out to play.'

Jim came to the phone and said, 'Hello, Bill. Do you want to play at home or away? You know me, I'm game for either.'

That was his way of putting Anna in her place. Smile and Overturn the Metaphor. SOM for short. It was a technique he used with deadly effect in Dáil debates, much to the discomfit of the witless leader of the opposition.

All this, flashing through his mind, only steeled him against her mockery.

'I'm convinced Jim has been kidnapped by the New Invincibles.'

'Tirra lirra, by the river, sang Sir Lancelot,' she responded.

For a moment he wondered if she'd been drinking. There was no point in trying to talk sense to her. She was determined to be awkward, or perhaps she really had three sheets to the wind.

'I'll keep my ear to the ground, Anna,' he said. 'I'll be in touch when I hear something.'

He put down the phone and shook his head. Jim used to say that she was a bit cuckoo. At the time he thought he was only joking. Now he was not so sure.

11

Woody was in bed with Jane when their lovemaking was interrupted by a four-note tinkle. She was lying on her back and he was lying on top of her. 'How can you?' she said as he reached for his mobile. Of all people, it was Sweetman at the other end.

'You're a genius, Woody. You predicted it all.'

'What?'

'Haven't you heard the news? MacBride's gone missing. The police are looking for him everywhere.'

'Sorry, I'm in the middle of something. Can I ring you back in half an hour?'

'Who was that?' Jane demanded.

'Sweetman.'

'Not the telly Sweetman, surely?'

'The very man.'

'You must be gone on him. You came off in me as soon as you heard his voice.'

'He had nothing to do with it. You squeezed on me suddenly. It was all your own fault.'

'That's right, blame me for your unpredictable little ding-a-ling.'

'Oh dear. It's going to be one of those Sundays, is it?'

'We'll have a snooze now and try again in half an hour. And next time turn off your mobile before you start.'

He knew he wouldn't sleep. MacBride was on his mind, and he kept asking himself if this was one of Sweetman's jokes. Jane, who had her back to him, had begun to snore softly, and for that he felt grateful. He looked at his watch and promised himself to let her sleep for at least an hour, by which time he would be fit for the fray again.

He slipped out of bed and stole downstairs to the living room, poured himself a glass of wine, and phoned Sweetman.

'Have you any idea where he could have gone?' Sweetman asked.

'Your guess is as good as mine.'

'I think he's joined Maguire.'

'On a distant cloud?'

'In Paris, where else? They're both very partial to a spot of sandwich sex and my courtesan is the very lady to provide it. She as good as told me so.'

'MacBride was the very picture of relaxed bonhomie when I met him last week.'

'He must have known we were on his tail and that it was only a matter of time before he was rumbled. The police were on to him as well. There may be some question of financial irregularities.'

He had another glass of wine and stole upstairs again. Slowly, he lifted the coverlet and slipped softly into bed. He was worried about MacBride and his own innocent role in the latest turn of events. If he hadn't mentioned MacBride to Sweetman, MacBride would not have been shadowed and he wouldn't have felt under pressure. Was there a malign agency at work, using him as its unsuspecting agent? No, that was ridiculous. There was neither a benign nor a malign force in the world—only blind humanity, muddling along as usual.

Jane turned in her sleep. She was now lying on her back, puffing gently as she breathed. She had a lovely profile. He was particularly fond of her nose, neck and ears. She was a great girl, none better, and she was now at her best with her reductive mind switched off. Her mind was the problem. It reduced everything, including what she called his ding-a-ling, to half its true size. But in time she would mellow, he hoped, and then they would live together in as much bliss as any couple could expect. Marital bliss was a romantic piece of fiction. How could any two people be happy in each other's company all the time? Now if Jane had Anna's mind, she would be perfect. But then she wouldn't be Jane. The world was full of women lacking in some vital ingredient. Even Sweetman's courtesan was hardly perfect. More than likely she could throw a tantrum with the best of them, but she obviously knew a trick or two that Anna Maguire and Maggie MacBride could not even begin to imagine. He was wondering what that trick might be when Jane turned on her side and they were locked once again in the age-old battle.

Mercifully, she declared his performance 'A1,' her highest mark of approbation. He had switched off his mobile and concentrated all his efforts on giving her a good time, in recognition of the principle of procrastinated ejaculation.

'That was perfect,' she said with a saucy flick of the tongue. 'You see, when you're with me you must forget all about Sweetman.'

'Sweetman has nothing to do with it. As far as I'm concerned, he's a nuisance. Never mention him to me again.'

'I won't mention him by name. I'll just call him the Unmentionable.'

'He keeps pestering me for new ideas. He's one of those men who want to know what everyone else is thinking because they don't know how to think for themselves.'

'If ever you don't know what to think, just ask me. But now I'm going to wait on you, hand and foot. What would you like for dinner?'

He fancied bangers and mash with onion rings and gravy, but even more he fancied a long evening on his own. She could do casseroled bangers to beat the band, but that would take well over an hour and possibly make her wish for more sex because of the suggestible nature of her mind.

'We had a heavy lunch; I'm not all that hungry,' he said. 'I'll open another bottle of wine and we'll have a glass or two with cream crackers and cheese. I've got some very nice Pont l'Évêque.'

'I have a feeling you're trying to sell me something.'

'Sell you something? I bought it especially for you.'

'Do you ever think about what's lacking in your life?' she asked when he had poured the wine.

'Not really. I'm happy enough, most of the time. I have no problems that a liberal injection of capital wouldn't solve.'

'I think of all the things we could be doing together.'

Alarmed by the direction the conversation had taken, he sought to steer clear of the danger.

'We've spent the afternoon doing together the very thing we most enjoy doing,' he smiled.

'We meet once a week for eight hours, five of which we spend in bed. It's so mechanical, and so lacking in imagination and originality.'

'We're both busy in our separate ways. Scraping a few euros together takes up most of my day.'

'You spend more time with other men in pubs than you spend with me.'

'I'm a freelance journalist. I can't rely on a fat cheque every month. What you call "men in pubs" is my main source of information.'

'You don't need to spend six evenings a week in the pub. We could devote a few evenings to each other, and I don't mean testing the bed springs.'

'I always thought you were a happy-go-lucky sort,' he said, a slight edge in his voice.

'I am happy, but I could be happier.'

'I'm pleased to hear it. People who are born miserable remain miserable. Happiness is a gift of the fairy godmother.'

'We could go swimming one evening a week, and another evening we could go jogging,' she said, returning to the fray.

'I'm not the athletic type, I'm afraid,' he said with an air of dismissal.

'If you're not the athletic type, you must be the scholarly type. We could learn a foreign language together.'

'English, for example.' He raised his glass. 'I'll drink to that.'

'I meant Italian. I love the sound of Italian and Pavarotti singing. We could go to Italy on holiday and call Florence Firenze.'

She was making a nuisance of herself, and he was itching to be rid of her. 'Bugger!' he said as the phone rang, while blessing whoever was at the other end.

'Who was that?' she asked when he'd put the phone down.

'Anna Maguire. She doesn't know when to stop.'

'One of the many women in your life.'

'Only one of them matters. You, Jane.'

'Then perhaps I should start pestering you like all the others.'

He was worried about Jane because she had all the court cards in her hand. She had made him feel that he had been short-changing her, and for that he could hardly blame her.

'If you're not doing anything on Wednesday, we could meet for dinner,' he offered.

'And where is dinner?'

'We could meet in the Long Hall for a drink and take it from there. Or you could come here and try out my *spaghetti alla carbonara*.'

'If you cook, I'll have to sing for my super. There will be no conversation. We'll drink too much wine and end up as we always do, testing the bed springs.'

'And what's wrong with that?'

'I want to talk to you. I want to get to know you. I want to feel that I'm part of your thinking and not just your humping life.'

'Fair enough. So what do you propose?'

'We'll meet in the Stag's Head for a drink at six. I know a little restaurant off Wicklow Street where we won't meet any newshounds or nosy parkers.'

'Done!' he said, knowing that for once she had got the better of him.

12

He had misled Jane because it was the sensible thing to do. He could not tell her that the woman who phoned in the middle of their conversation was an old flame, Louise Lamotte. He disliked himself for telling a barefaced lie, but it would have made no sense to introduce another quantity into the equation already balanced so delicately in her mind. Jane didn't mind Anna Maguire. She had seen her with Maguire and knew that she was too seasoned to be a serious threat. For that reason she was more or less content to accept the situation. Louise Lamotte was in her thirties, and a few years younger than Jane. Even hinting that such a woman had once been part of his life would light a fuse leading directly to a rather large powder keg.

Louise was his Dark Lady, but only in a sense peculiar to him. She had lovely pale skin and black hair, and she looked as if her mother could have been Spanish, though as far as he could tell both her parents were Irish. When he first caught a glimpse of her he had been recuperating from his infatuation with Anna, and felt that here, surely, was the girl with the cure. He devoted two precious years of his young life to dreaming about her and making up the conversations he would have with her if ever they should meet. When finally they became close, she led him a shameless dance. They used to meet for a drink and what she called 'off-the-wall' conversation, until finally he discovered that all the time she was having a torrid affair with a well-heeled vet. The knowledge that she had been using him as a kind of *amuse-gueule* broke his heart. He was still plunging about in the sinking sands of melancholia when Jane came to his rescue. He never mentioned Louise. Instead, he blamed his black humour on the uncertainties of freelance journalism, for which by temperament he was ill-suited.

Jane accepted him at face value. In her no-nonsense way she took him in hand and made him whole again. She wasn't the romantic type. She didn't seem at all interested in love, or even sex. She behaved as if their relationship were a matter of practical common sense. She ironed his shirts and darned his socks and took the trouble to make him look 'half-decent', as she put it. When they ended up in bed together one evening, there was no one more surprised than he. Even their lovemaking seemed no more than a common or garden pursuit, the sort of thing that wasn't far removed from the ironing of shirts and the darning of socks. In his early twenties he would have seen such a relationship as laughable, but within months she had given him back his self-esteem, and for that he could only be grateful. Now he could not imagine a life without her.

As soon as she had gone, he phoned Louise.

'What are you up to these days?' she asked.

'Nothing much. Mainly 'ritin' and readin'. I don't stretch to 'rithmetic.'

'I liked your piece on Maguire. As it happens, I know a lady who was very close to him. It occurred to me that you might like to meet her.'

'It would depend on how well she knew him and on what she has to say.'

'They met mainly in bed, she says. I must warn you that she isn't among his most ardent admirers; their relationship ended too abruptly for her liking.'

'I wouldn't be interested in a tabloid kiss-and-tell job.'

'She has unusual insights, and she feels the time has come to tell her story.'

'For "tell" she probably means "sell",' he said.

'Do you know anyone who might be interested?'

'I'll tell you that when I've heard the story.'

'Why don't you come round to my place for dinner? I'm dying to hear your news. I've often wondered how you were getting on.'

They settled for Tuesday, the day before he was due to meet Jane again. He didn't know what to make of Louise. She sounded so mysterious, but he was curious to see how she was weathering and to learn more about the Rubik's cube that was Jim Maguire's life. He wouldn't be prepared to write a cheap 'we-always-met-in-bed' story, but from a personal point of view he would enjoy hearing the prurient details. They might even bring a little grist to his mill as the great man's self-appointed biographer.

He kept recalling Louise throughout the evening. Talking to her had reopened a wound he thought had healed. Again and again he asked himself why she had invited him to dinner. She could just as easily have given him her friend's phone number and have done with it. In spite of how he felt, he would meet her and give nothing of himself away. She had phoned out of curiosity, and he had accepted her invitation out of curiosity. They would sit on either side of the fireplace while he listened sceptically to her attempts to interest him in the fret and ferment of her two-timing life. She had made a fool of him once; she would not make a fool of him again.

He remembered her as 'svelte of limb and smoothly gliding'. That was how he described her in an embarrassing piece of doggerel he once wrote for her birthday. How many times had he sat at the back of the hall while she glided up and down the catwalk and older men gazed admiringly at her in the front? How many times had he wondered what she could see in an impecunious journalist? Surely, it must be true love, he'd told himself. In his self-admiring naïvety her 'love' had deluded him into thinking he was strong. Jane had given him a different strength, nothing less than strength of mind.

He was about to settle down to a book when Anna rang. Sweetman had been in touch to let her know that he would love to write Jim's biography and to ask if he could rely on her help.

'The cheek of the man!' she said. 'After all the claptrap he's talked and written! I told him that it was too early to immortalise Jim; that we should first allow the journalistic dust to settle. As a parting shot, I told him that I was sure the authorised biography would be written by a professional historian with access to all the necessary papers. He wouldn't be put off. He says he wants to strike while the iron is hot.'

'No one can stop him if he means business. He's got access to every newspaper file since the day Jim entered the Dáil. With his army of researchers, he can cobble something together in a matter of months.'

'All he's interested in is sensationalism, and I know he won't be deterred by me. That's why I'd like to talk to you. Are you free to come round for a drink tomorrow evening? I won't call it a "preprandial" because that was Jim's word.'

He said he could come at around six, while at the back of his mind was the knowledge that she might easily begin to make a nuisance of herself. Still, it was in his interest to keep her sweet. She meant well. Her aim was to ensure that Jim would be remembered for his life rather than his unexplained death.

As he cycled up the gravelled avenue, he felt pleased that Jane could not see him. Her fault-seeking mind would have delighted in the incongruity of his shabby jacket and the formality of the approach. Even the pleached lime trees on either side looked like wary sentries, alert and ready to eject any insincere visitors.

Anna led him into Jim's study, an airy, high-ceilinged room with two tall bookcases and three big windows. His desk was in the centre of the floor with two windows behind and another at the side. There was a sideboard, two leather armchairs and a chaise longue, on which lay a neatly folded tartan blanket.

'Jim used to call the chaise longue his day-bed,' she smiled. 'He loved to stretch out on it and read. He spent hours on his own in this room. It was here he did his thinking, never in the cut and thrust of conversation with colleagues. He just bounced ideas off them, and then came back here for the kind of pondering that ends in a decision. He wrote all his speeches at that desk. This was his sanctum, though he never called it that. Jokingly, he used to refer to it as the wheel-house. He rarely invited any of his friends in here, except MacBride. Sit in his chair if you want to see what I mean. You might even get an insight into the way his mind worked.'

'I could pretend to be Taoiseach for five minutes!' He smiled as he sat in Maguire's high-backed chair, and again thanked heavens that Jane could not see him. He stretched his legs and clasped his hands over the large blotting pad. Before him was a laptop, on one side of which lay *The Chambers Dictionary* and *The Oxford Dictionary of Quotations*. On the other side stood a card on which was printed a quotation from Charles de Gaulle.

'So this is all you need to run the country!' he said.

'It was all Jim needed. He probably read that quotation every day.'

It was nothing to write home about. He felt he could have done better himself.

In politics it is necessary to betray one's country or the electorate.
I prefer to betray the electorate.

– Charles de Gaulle

The quotation must have resonated with Maguire, providing as it did an excellent excuse for double-talk and broken promises. He thought it advisable not to share his thoughts with Anna.

'Do you fancy a wee dram?' she asked, going to the sideboard.

'I wouldn't say no to what my father used to call a ball of malt.' He rose from Maguire's chair.

'We'll try the Jameson. It's the sweetest. Water?'

'No, I take after my father. He began putting water in his only when he turned eighty.'

'Here's to Jim. If he's still alive, I hope he's happy.' She raised her glass.

When they'd drunk to Jim and his happiness, he said that it was lovely whiskey in order to take her mind off her favourite subject.

'It's Redbreast,' she said. 'It should be good. But I have a confession to make. I asked you here for a purpose. I was wondering if you'd like to write a biography of Jim, something to counter Sweetman's scandal-mongering.'

'A balancing of the books, you mean?'

'It would only be an interim account. It's too early to write the full history.'

'Sweetman has the advantage. He has helpers to call on. As a freelance, I'd be delving laboriously on my own.'

She wondered how much she should tell him. One way or another she would have to take him into her confidence. He was fond of her once. He was not the kind of man who would let her down.

'I can help you there. Jim left several boxes of notes and documents as well as a detailed journal. He obviously had hoped to write his memoirs one day. You would have to work in this room, of course. I wouldn't want anything removed from here in case it might get lost or fall into the wrong hands.'

'It's a tricky one. I'd love to write something about Jim, but earning a living takes up most of my time. At best I could come here only two mornings a week.'

'Let's try it out and see how you go.'

She mentioned her study on the first floor, and said that it was there she did all her writing, and that he would have Jim's study to himself. There would be no one to disturb him, except possibly the home help, who came on Mondays and Fridays.

'Surroundings are half the battle for a writer. Here you will find yourself inspired. I know you'll write something witty and lively, something that sees through the low cloud into the high blue heavens beyond.'

He did not tell her that he was already writing a biography of Jim, and that all he had to do was to complete the last chapter. Neither did he tell her that she talked a lot of bollocks, which was something her younger self never did. If only Anna Harvey at twenty could have heard Anna Maguire at fifty! Perhaps she'd had a few Redbreasts before he arrived. She wouldn't be the first widow to seek solace in the bottle.

He told her that he had a meeting at eight. In spite of everything, he felt excited. For once he would have the advantage over Sweetman. As he freewheeled back down the avenue, the lime trees looked less stiff and sentry-like. Perhaps he only imagined it, but they seemed to be linking arms in cheerful fellowship.

13

The story of MacBride's disappearance occupied the front page of every morning paper. It was a gift from heaven, a mystery that every journalist, however lowly, felt qualified to solve. The ground had been well prepared; MacBride's name had already been linked with Maguire's. The story practically wrote itself, and what is more, it demanded to be written in a certain way. Everyone assumed that MacBride's disappearance could only be viewed as the ineluctable concomitant of the disappearance of his friend. A preordained pattern had emerged, and the elements of the pattern differed only in incidental particulars. One paper argued that the New Invincibles were behind the disappearance of both men, while another suggested that for years Maguire and MacBride had enjoyed a financially symbiotic relationship, and that understandably they'd now gone abroad to enjoy the fruits of their ill-gotten gains. Yet another, reaching further downmarket, claimed that one of Maguire's former mistresses had been seen boarding a flight to Paris on the day MacBride disappeared. It showed pictures of her, MacBride and Maguire in happier times above a caption that read, 'Sandwich Anyone?'

Woody had arranged to spend the morning chez Maguire. He was looking forward to seeing what was on offer in the way of sources, and the level of detail and analysis in Maguire's journal. However, the diary was the last thing on Anna's mind.

'First things first,' she said firmly. 'You've seen the morning papers? We have to do something about this wild speculation. It would be nothing short of libellous if both men were still alive.' At last she had acknowledged the possibility that Maguire might be dead. She then listed all the things his piece should cover, counting on the fingers of both hands.

'Journalism doesn't work like that,' he told her. 'To get published these days, an article must have cutting edge. I'll have to put on an attitude of knowingness and flea-market cynicism. The reading public want conspiracy, chicanery and sex, and they must be satisfied.'

'Surely you're not telling me that it's the readers who write the news?'

'They don't write it day to day, but in the long run they determine which newspapers attract advertising and therefore survive.'

'For once, don't worry about the long run. Write a piece for Jim and me. If you do, I won't forget it.'

She went to her study, leaving him alone in the lofty room. He felt something of a fraud seated behind the great man's desk. There was a ghost behind the curtains that kept mocking him, and Jane stood at his elbow, taunting him and scoffing at his dubious motives. If only he could find the first sentence, the second and the third might come. Essentially, there were four different angles and he needed to think up a linking thread that no one else had thought of. In the end he decided to give the mare her head; to ride with both eyes closed and hope she wouldn't end up in the ditch. He would write long and edit short. After an hour he read over what he'd written, which was far too academic to fool a prurient news editor. He got to work again, cutting mercilessly and introducing a spicy morsel in each paragraph as he went along. At last he had to accept that it was the best he could do in the circumstances.

Anna's study door was closed. He knocked, waiting for her to open it, and when she did he handed her his essay as if she were his tutor. He stood by the door with one hand on the knob and watched her face while she read.

'It isn't what I would have written, but what I would have written wouldn't get published,' she said. 'You've pulled the chestnuts out of the fire, and I won't forget it.'

'I must warn you that it may not be published as it stands; it's bound to be mauled. And more than likely it will appear under a misleading headline.'

'We've done our best. It's all we can do. Next time you come I'll have the boxes ready for you, and the journal.'

'I'll come on Thursday, since the home help won't be around.'

'Jim used to say that realpolitik was the bane of his life. Has any journalist ever said to you that facts were the bane of his?'

'I don't think so.'

'What would you call a journalist who only dealt in facts? Unemployable?'

'Possibly a science correspondent,' he smiled.

'You must stay for dinner on Thursday. We'll try some more of the Redbreast. Jim left a whole case of it.'

'What if he comes back and fancies a dram or two himself?'

'I'll tell him it was drunk in a good cause.'

He couldn't imagine what had got into her. While Jim was around she had contrived to fade into the background, gliding silently from room to room, smiling dutifully at her husband's jokes, and speaking out only when he said something outrageous for effect. She had found her voice, but not her old voice. She was her own woman at last, but not the woman he once knew and loved. He was biased, of course. He would never see her with Jane's unblinking eye. If they ever met, she and Jane would have something pertinent to say about each other. But such a meeting was inconceivable—Jane would be jealous if she knew that he and Anna were old friends. He would have to make her see that, as Maguire's biographer, he had every reason to cultivate the goodwill of his widow. Otherwise, how could he gain access to the documents and journal on which the success of his book depended? Jane was nothing if not practical; she was bound to understand.

On the way home his thoughts turned to Louise Lamotte and her invitation to dinner. As a man who valued the simple life as much as he valued the linear narrative in journalism, he began to regret having accepted. He first knew Louise as Jo Malacky, a girl of nineteen, still talking about her convent education and the overbearing nuns who had been sitting on her for the previous five years. She was determined to 'break out,' as she put it; to make up as fast as possible for the years of empty novenas and cold devotions. 'I want to fill my life with movement,' she'd told him. 'I want to travel. I don't want to rot like a cabbage in a back garden.' He found her a job in a typing pool, which she held down for less than a month. She was soon modelling teenage fashions for catalogues, which she said would tide her over until 'something big' turned up. Within a year she was on the catwalk, which turned out to be her natural home. She had become a lingerie model, and for professional reasons had changed her name to Louise Lamotte. 'You can still call me Jo,' she told him, 'but I'd rather you called me Louise. It's more me.'

He rang the doorbell and looked up at the stained-glass fanlight. She opened the door and smiled.

'Kevin!' she exclaimed. 'How lovely to see you!' She had put on her best theatrical voice for him.

She was in her thirties now. She'd filled out, but hadn't lost her figure. She still looked attractive, though her hair and skin had lost some of the lustre and bloom he remembered. As she led the way up the stairs to her flat, he had ample opportunity to observe her perfect legs and dainty little bottom. On the landing she turned and faced him. 'Over the years I've often thought of you. I always read your Sunday column, and whenever I do, your voice rings again in my ear.'

Her living room was cosy, with old-fashioned furniture and uplights illuminating the enlarged photographs on the walls showing her in various moods. In one she was smiling, in a second serious, and in a third pensively studying a wilting rose.

'I come back here to be myself,' she said. 'I never feel at home in the public eye.' She was talking like a politician rather than a model. Perhaps she could count more than one politician among her friends.

'I've been out all day,' she confided. 'I haven't had time to cook dinner. We'll have a glass of Chianti and a pizza, if you don't mind.'

'A pizza and a glass of Chianti would be perfect.'

'You see, I haven't forgotten. I remember how fond you were of Italian cuisine.'

She poured the wine, and they talked about what she called old times. She asked him about his work and the journalists he knew, and she told him about what she had been doing since they last met. After half an hour the doorbell rang. She went downstairs and came back with two flat boxes containing two pizzas.

'I like my pizzas hot,' she said, as they sat down on opposite sides of the circular table.

His thoughts kept darting in all directions. He was finding it difficult to concentrate. 'I like your table,' he said, hoping to keep the conversation impersonal.

'I bought it some years ago at a Big House auction. I like round tables. They give everyone the same weight and value. No one can complain about being seated below the salt.'

It was at least ten years since he'd last had a pizza; they always gave him heartburn and constipation. This one was only lukewarm and it weighed heavily in his gut, but still he ate manfully and complimented her on her choice. They had exhausted all the obvious topics. It was time to get down to what his editor would call 'the meat of the thing'.

'Who is the lady you mentioned over the phone?' he finally asked.

'Which lady?'

'The one who knew Maguire.'

'Surely you must have guessed! It's your old heart-throb, yours truly.'

'I thought Maguire went to Paris for his fun.'

'He found his *Folies Bergère* right here.'

'Is that what you wanted to tell me?'

'Only part of it. You see, I've outgrown the catwalk. I'm now planning to become an actress. I'm just the right age for all the great roles. I've always wanted to write a book. It would add weight to my CV. I've got all the right ideas, but I've never been trained to write them down. I need a ghostwriter, not any old hack but someone who knows me, preferably an old friend, someone I can talk to freely about my memories, and someone who knows which questions to ask and won't be afraid to ask them. I need a good journalist like you.'

'I can put you in touch with one or two ghostwriters.'

'It needn't take up much of your time, Kevin. We could meet here a few times a week with a tape recorder. I could ad lib and you could ask me questions. The names that come up will surprise you.'

'I've never written a book. You need someone who does ghosting for a living.'

'I was hoping you'd do it as a favour for old times' sake. I'm not well off. We could come to some arrangement about the royalties, and of course I'd be only too happy to help you in any other way you fancy—I know a lot of people who might be of use to you.'

She poured more wine, and he told her he felt certain that she had an interesting story to tell.

'You see, I feel at home with you. I often think about the past and wish I had it back. I was very young and green when I first knew you, but you taught me things I never forgot.'

She was getting personal, and he felt uncomfortable. He knew he had to make his escape.

'Let me think about it for a few days,' he said.

She got up and went to the coffee table. She picked up a book and flopped down on the sofa. 'Come and have a look at this,' she said. 'Strange how some things survive.'

He stood looking down at the postcard in her hand. He could see that her lovely hair had lost its bounce from too many rinses. The flower that once hath blown. She patted the sofa and smiled. Dutifully, he sat beside her.

'This is the card you sent me for my twenty-first. I came across it in a bundle of old letters the other day.' She had thought of everything, it would seem; she had everything so conveniently to hand.

'Let me read it to you in my best actress voice:

Let hawks come down from the air.
Let queens die young and fair.
I'll love Louise forevermore.'

'Did I send you that?'

'Look, it's your handwriting.'

'It was a long time ago. I have no recollection of it.'

'It's a lovely little poem.'

'It isn't original. It's a kind of medley.'

'A melody in words. What a lovely thought! I was too young to appreciate you at the time. I'm a different person now. I'm deep, or so I've been told. I have deep thoughts, and deep things to say about life. I like to read the interviews that actresses give—they are so shallow and so self-centred. I'm more interested in other people than in myself. I'm no longer the playful little kitten you used to know. My only regret is that I didn't read enough books, but in spite of that I've enjoyed my life, and the best of it is still to come. I'm on the brink of something new, and I know it will be something big.'

He couldn't just get up and go. He needed to find a natural pause in the conversation or a friendly note to end on. 'How do you see your life?' he asked. 'What's the storyline?'

'I'm on an up-escalator and I'm now halfway to the top.'

'Where is the yeast that will cause the dough to rise?'

'You see, that's why I need you as my ghost. I've got all the ideas but none of the words. There's nothing in life I haven't come across. I've learnt a lot from the people I've met—politicians, solicitors, doctors, professors, architects, even one or two priests and—would you believe it?—a bishop. They used to ask me questions that made me think, and I used to ask them questions about how they felt. I've never had a shallow relationship with any man. The catwalk is fascinating, but it's for youngsters. Now I need to express my whole personality and give readers the benefit of my experience. What do you think?'

'You need to find the thread that will hold your story together. Otherwise it will be about spilling the beans, one bean after another.' He wished to say that it isn't easy distinguishing between beans, but he was not a man who liked giving offence.

'You're very hard on me, Kevin, but I know you don't mean it.' She leant over and smiled into his face.

'Give me a week or so to think about it. I'm sure I can come up with something.' He got to his feet and thanked her for a lovely evening. 'I have to go now. I must knock off a review before bedtime. It's prosaic, I know, but it's my bread and butter.'

She got up and took his hand. 'I really enjoyed seeing you again, Kevin. I was an innocent when we met. It was you who taught me how to kiss. You led me down the primrose path, you devil. Let me kiss you for old times' sake.'

It wasn't a long kiss. It was the kind of kiss a devoted wife might give her departing husband at a railway station: short, but not perfunctory.

'Did that remind you of anything?' she smiled.

'I could stand a lot of those.' He opened the door.

He was so pleased to have escaped that he was halfway home before he became aware that her kiss was still on his lips. And not just on his lips but imprinted on his whole sexual being. She had awakened something that had been sleeping in the unexplored recesses of his mind. She had lit a lamp that glowed inside him, illuminating dreams and impossible desires. They were not his desires, but the desires of an ancestor he thought he had disowned.

He spent a restless night, so disturbed in his body that he could not sleep. He asked himself if he had lost his inner equilibrium or whatever it was that caused his life to flow evenly from hour to hour and from one day to the next. He emptied his mind of every human image and imagined a gyroscope inside his skull that kept his thoughts revolving evenly and his mind from listing. When finally he found rest, it was to dream, not about Louise but Jane. He woke at eight, late for him, grateful for the cold logic of a new day. He had been the victim of a Chianti-inspired fantasy. She had wrecked his happiness once before. On no account must he allow her to wreck it again.

14

She had promised Woody to get everything ready for his next visit. She had looked through Jim's journal and found it heavy going. Nothing but politics and policies, cabinet meetings, who said this and who said that. The dry-as-dust tone was untypical of the man. It read as if he had gone through life without ever discovering his true vocation. Even in their early days on the magazine she could tell that he was different. He was imaginative and original. Unlike other men, he did not keep telling her things she'd already read in the Sunday review pages. When he told her that he was planning to stand for election to the Dáil, she was deeply disappointed. She had already mapped out for him a more original, certainly a less pedestrian, career.

On the magazine, Woody wrote most of the articles but it was Jim who came up with the ideas. Jim was too fastidious to succeed at journalism, too ready to ponder over the exact meaning of a word. His heart was set on politics. He told her that his ambition was to 'give a leg-up to the little man from Ringsend or Ballyhuppachaun at the expense of the well-heeled toff from Killiney.' That was typical of Jim. He would have no truck with phrases like 'the redistribution of wealth'; when he talked economics, he talked about people he knew. Listening to him, she often felt that he didn't need to read the papers to keep in touch; that he carried the needs of ordinary people around with him in his heart and head.

After work they used to meet for drinks, unbeknown to Woody, when he would stretch his legs and give free play to his mind. He was half a dozen men in one, each of them at loggerheads with the others: man of action *v.* scholar-bibliophile; social charmer *v.* solitary contemplative; artist *v.* would-be politician. It was that aspect of him that she'd found fascinating; she'd seen it as her duty to take him in hand and create order from the chaos of his private antinomies. He used to say that he should have been born into the nomadic life, sleeping under desert stars and letting his camel choose the way. He admired the great adventurers. His heroes were Marco Polo, Shackleton and Scott. He liked to think that he had more in common with these men than with any politician, living or dead. Small wonder that the Irish people didn't understand him. They voted for him reluctantly rather than wholeheartedly, condemning him to a life of looking over his shoulder at men he despised. At times it was painful to see the suffering in his face. She could understand why he used to talk fondly about the eighteenth-century enlightened despots of Europe. He particularly admired Joseph II and his enthusiasm for music and the arts. Though he never voiced such thoughts in public, he often said that he regretted the cultural ignorance of his fellow politicians. Over dinner he used to recall that the old Irish chieftains had their own bards. Then he'd laugh and say that perhaps he should have his own harpist like Fionn Mac Cumhaill.

In the early years of their life together she felt privileged in having such a rare man for a husband. When she began writing and publishing, she realised that marriage to him had condemned her to life in the shadows. How could she tell him that she longed for just one day alone in the sun?

She had decided that Woody should work in the study, where he might have a sense of intimacy with Jim's way of thinking and perhaps even a sense of being in a special place. He would be free to look at the books that had furnished Jim's mind, proving that he was not just another philistine politician out to feather his own nest. She looked around the room to make sure that it contained nothing unfit for a journalist's eye to see. Finally, she went to the drinks cabinet to inspect the single malts. There was a half-full bottle of Highland Park, which she had not sampled before. Reaching for it, she noticed that the space inside the cabinet was not as deep as she had expected, which seemed odd to say the least.

She removed all the bottles and discovered what looked like a sliding door. She opened it to find up to twelve moleskin notebooks stacked one on top of the other. As they were only three inches wide, they fitted perfectly into the small space. She looked through one or two of them without stopping to read; they were nothing less than a personal diary in Jim's neat hand—an odd sort of diary, full of abbreviations and symbols meant only for the eyes of the writer. Feeling a surge of excitement, she removed all the notebooks and put the bottles back in their place. She poured herself a large Highland Park and sat down at the desk to read.

The diary, which was an uninhibited confession, began eleven years ago, after they'd moved to Howth. It contained his private thoughts—thoughts he wouldn't dream of airing in company, and certainly not in hers. She couldn't imagine why he had written it except possibly as a safety valve, a means of blowing off steam. She had the impression that his whole public life had been a denial of his true nature; that he had lived a lie from start to finish; that he had never uttered a word of the truth before. At first she felt guilty for trespassing on his privacy, but soon her guilt turned to anger and shame as she realised that she knew nothing of the man she had been married to for almost thirty years. She had known only the public man, the passionate man on the platform, the man the electorate knew. He had shut a door in her face. He had been closer to the least of his mistresses than he'd ever been to her. The one he referred to as 'L' he called 'my lovely Miss Kisscock' because she was so good at ministering to his peculiar need. She found herself weeping uncontrollably. With a shaking hand she poured herself another whisky, trying to breathe deeply so as to calm down. He had humiliated her behind her back. He had forced her to live a lie, to live the life of a contented woman who thought the world of her husband and who was happy to allow him a certain amount of lenity because, as she used to put it to herself, 'boys will be boys'. Now she knew what he'd really thought of her:

'I am on a political treadmill by day and a domestic treadmill at night. Anna, God help us, is absorbed in her fairy tales. She talks to me as if I were a child, or worse, a naughty boy. What am I to do? No ease at home, no peace in the Kremlin. I am the captain of a ship tossed at sea. My life is no longer my own to control.'

The Kremlin was what he called the seat of government, Leinster House. As a young man, his whole ambition was to make his mark there. Having got to the top of the tree, he could only complain that the tree wasn't tall enough. Nothing could ever please his restless and insatiable nature. None of that was beyond the bounds of her understanding. What she could neither understand nor forgive was his shameful sexual life, which degraded her as well as himself. If any of it should ever come to light, what would his admirers make of it?

Obviously, he was searching for something she could not begin to imagine. It could not have been crude sex, which was Miss Kisscock's department. Whatever it was, he was convinced that only young women had it. The diary described one of his many visits to Paris when he was taken to a nightclub by his

French host. He was so bewitched by the voice of a young singer that he couldn't get her out of his mind. He told himself that by lunchtime the following day he would have forgotten all about her, but when lunchtime came he could still hear her voice in his ear. He had always treasured what he called 'the authenticity of the moment'. He was convinced that all falsehood sprang from recollection, and he was determined to prove himself right. The following evening he went back to the nightclub on his own to talk to the singer. She sang 'Danny Boy' in French, and with such feeling that she brought tears to his eyes. She had sung it for him alone, he felt. Worse, he was convinced that if only he could make love to her he would gain access to the self-knowledge that an unsatisfactory life had denied him. It was the beginning of one of his many hopeless 'love' affairs. In many ways he was a child, which is why he used to enjoy her fairy tales in the early years of their life together. He used to say that, unlike the world of the Kremlin, her stories were perfect. Again, she found herself weeping.

Why did he do it? Why did he need to do it when he was so close to perfection in every other way?

But perhaps it was all sexual fantasising, an attempt at wish-fulfilment by a man who was so busy with politics that he had lost touch with his masculine nature and how to express it like any normal man. Some patriots believed that the Casement diaries were no more than the wild imaginings of an unworldly idealist. Perhaps the same could be said about Jim's. But she had to admit that the cutting references to her shortcomings as a wife were no fantasies. Turning a page, she came across her name again:

Anna has aged in advance of her years. By forty she had lost whatever interest she once had in sexual self-expression. Not that she was ever one for a rough-and-tumble houghmagandy. Even in her short-lived salad days she gave an impression of prim toleration rather than avid participation. Sex is something you need to go at wholeheartedly. Any woman who goes to bed to agonise and psychologise should never have got married to a red-blooded man. Anna's problem is that she can't turn off her interrogatory mind, an echo chamber of "don'ts" and "must nots". She lives in the world of Goldilocks and Little Red Riding Hood. I even caught her the other day reading a book about Little Red Riding Hood. Thank heavens for Little Miss Kisscock, whose name I pronounce Kiss-Co for the sake of propriety. She keeps me from losing what's left of my mind.

She closed the notebook and burst into tears again. How could he be so cruel to her after all she'd done for him, washing and ironing, cooking and sewing, looking after his every need? She could not bear to read another word. Rather shakily, she poured a whisky and took it to her bedroom. She was still weeping when she got into bed.

15

The journal volumes were laid out on the desk in readiness, the boxes of letters and documents stacked by the wall.

'I'll trust you not to remove anything and not to photograph anything,' she said. 'Now I'll leave you to it. I usually have a slice of quiche and a glass of Chablis at one. You're more than welcome to join me, if you're still here.'

She looked somewhat severe, as if talking to a house party guest who had misbehaved with one of the chambermaids. He watched her as she went to the door, wondering if subconsciously he still felt socially inferior in her presence, which, of course, was quite preposterous. She'd never put on airs before. Perhaps she'd misinterpreted something he'd said. He told himself that he had work to do, and lowered his bottom into the late Taoiseach's chair.

Maguire had kept his journal in clothbound A4 notebooks. They were not the kind of notebooks one found in stationery shops; these had been specially bound to last. Written in a small, neat hand with neither blottings nor crossings out, the diary began on the day Maguire entered the Dáil and ended the day before he left for Conamara on his last known journey. Woody began at the beginning, and within an hour and a half he had glanced through all nine volumes, just to get the flavour. He paid particular attention to the last volume, which covered the weeks before Maguire's disappearance, but there was no mention of anything that might shed light on his state of mind. Where he had expected careful pondering and analysis, he found only what he would describe as the minutes of meetings held, including what each participant had said, but without a word about what any of them must have thought but did not say. In fact, the journal could have been the work of a stenographer or secretary intent on giving everyone his due without reference to either motive or ambition. Curiously, there was no reference to Maguire's own reflections or motives either. He simply stated what was in the interest of the country, as if the interest of the country must inevitably be his own. No attempt was made to enter into the minds of the other actors either, and no reference was made to the compromises and the wheeling and dealing at the heart of daily life in any coalition government with a slender majority. There was nothing that might delight the heart of a journalist in search of scandal or a biographer in search of a fresh insight. Maguire was no Greville, and certainly no Pepys.

He asked himself why he had kept such a journal. His motive could not have been self-justification because there was little or no attempt to defend the positions he had adopted on any of the questions presented. In fact there was nothing in the journal that would not become available when the state papers for the period were finally released. He felt disheartened, thwarted by the disappointment of high expectations. The Maguire of the journal was not just a cold fish but a fish that had come straight from the freezer—the antithesis of the passionate man he had been seeking to bring to life in his biography.

'Well, what do you think?' Anna asked as they sat down to their lunchtime snack. She had put on a little make-up, and she looked more relaxed. He wondered if he had merely imagined her earlier *froideur*.

'I spent the morning just copy tasting, scratching the surface rather than delving deep.'

'Find any gems?'

'Jim seems to have put very little of himself into his journal. He was a fiery orator when the occasion demanded; he could communicate passion and verve and still keep his cool. None of that comes across, I'm afraid. The journal could have been written by an accountant, but perhaps that is the impression he wished to leave behind.'

'Jim wasn't a writer. He wasn't an original thinker either. He was simply a man who knew how to get things done. He soaked up other people's ideas, and then rescued the grain from the chaff. Once when I asked him what he'd been doing in his study all evening, he just said, "winnowing". I knew precisely what he meant.'

'Winnowing is not a gift to be sneezed at. Every successful politician and businessman does it. Journalists are a dab hand at it.'

'Another thing Jim was good at was starting hares, and then sitting back gleefully to watch the opposition give chase.'

'He had a mischievous sense of humour, but none of that comes across either.'

'You'll have to fill in the gaps from your knowledge of him. You knew him before he became famous. In other words, you know him better than any other journalist around.'

She asked if he was planning to work through the afternoon. When he said yes, she said she was going into town to shop and that she'd be back around four.

He returned to the study and got down to work. He already knew the outline of the story and the sequence of events. He could not bring himself to begin tiresomely at the beginning, so he began at the end, hoping to work his way back. He heard the front door click closed. From the window he watched her get into her little Polo and drive down the avenue between the concatenated sentries. He had just come across the phrase 'a concatenation of mishaps' in the journal. Applying the word to the lime trees amused him, but only until he recalled Jane saying 'You're easily amused, Kevin,' followed by a hurtful laugh in which he pretended to join.

The relentless detail of the journal gave the impression of a life in which one thing followed another without rhyme or reason. He longed for what his editor called 'one gee-whiz insight', or at least an imaginative linking of one fact to another. What the journal lacked was imagination, the gift of metaphor that with a single whip-crack can weld two incongruous images or ideas and create a brand new universe. Impatiently, he rose from his swivel chair to inspect Maguire's bookshelves, hoping to gain an insight into a mind that seemed closed against all probing. With any luck he might be one of those readers who underlined phrases and scribbled rude comments in the margins.

One bookcase contained literary works, mainly English and French poetry and fiction with a few well-chosen specimens of literary criticism. The other bookcase contained works of history and political biography. There was a full shelf devoted to General de Gaulle, and on the top shelf a twelve-volume cabinet edition of Lecky's *History of England in the Eighteenth Century*. Wondering if Maguire had actually read the formidable work, he found himself glancing at the preface in which Lecky declares his intention 'to disengage from the great mass of facts those which relate to the permanent forces of the nation.' Clearly, that is what he himself would have to do with the diary: boil it down to give the life some semblance of shape and purpose. He would confer the benison of meaning where Maguire had seen none.

He returned the volume to its place and took down one of the volumes devoted to Ireland. The gap on the bookshelf revealed a black moleskin notebook lying on its fore-edge behind the Lecky volumes. With some difficulty he extracted it from its hiding place and opened it at random. As far as he could tell, it was a kind of diary written for Maguire's eyes only. It was full of symbols and abbreviations; it was perhaps what the Francophile Maguire might call a *journal intime*. Suddenly, the truth dawned on him: it was the real diary, a record of Maguire's sexual exploits giving locations, names and dates. His heart almost missed a beat. The record began in the previous September and ended abruptly a month before Maguire's disappearance. Quite possibly, the notebook was the last of a sequence, the one he had been writing up before the tragedy. But where were the others? He couldn't ask Anna. She would be utterly horrified if she knew.

The front door clicked open. It closed again with a bang that shook the floor beneath him. He slipped the notebook into his jacket pocket and resumed his labours on the journal as he listened to her tread on the stairs.

'Shopping is never-ending,' she said as she entered. 'It takes up a ridiculous amount of my time, but at least it gets me out of the house. How is the work going?'

'Slowly, I'm afraid. The journal never deviates from the trudge of political life. There is no mention of holidays or journeys made in leisure time. It's a record of meetings, nothing more. A biography based on the journal alone would not reveal the passionate politician, the man of flesh and blood we all knew.'

'What are you trying to tell me, Kevin?' She drew closer to the desk, as if challenging him to speak his mind, which was precisely what he proposed to do.

'If we limit the book to the politics of Kildare Street it will result in an inward-looking, dry-as-dust story that no one will want to read.'

'I think you know how to make politics exciting. You do it every day.'

'I see our book as a counterblast to Sweetman's. The gossip has it that he proposes to deliver next May for publication the following September and in good time for the Christmas market. He won't limit himself to the political life, I can assure you. He'll take every opportunity to produce a bestseller.'

'But what will he write about if not politics?'

'He'll rehash all the scandalous gossip already published in the newspapers, and above all he'll make Jim's disappearance the natural and predictable climax of the story. In fact, he may well begin his book with a detailed account of Jim's last day, and in subsequent chapters present a career leading inexorably to that ending.'

'But that's absurd!'

'It's journalism.'

'But how can you be so sure?'

'You've seen Sweetman on television and you've read his articles in the press. He has form, as he himself would say. I don't need to read his book. If I were sufficiently unscrupulous, I could write it.'

'So what do you suggest we do?'

'Produce something to counterbalance all the scandal-mongering and conspiracy theories. I think the way to lance the boil is to analyse every conceivable theory and show them all up as so much piffle. Above all we need to present Jim as a man of many gifts, with one or two natural flaws that kept him from achieving greatness.'

'I can see what you're getting at. Let me think about it. Next time you come, I'll cook dinner. We'll talk it over and hammer out a strategy.'

'I'll be off shortly,' he said. 'I must read a book I'm reviewing for Saturday.'

'Surely you won't read it in one sitting?'

'I hope to. The modest cheque I'll get for my labour wouldn't justify two.'

'New Grub Street is alive and well and thriving in Dublin!'

He couldn't wait to get to grips with the real diary. On the way home he bought some smoked salmon at the supermarket so that he wouldn't have to spend too much time in the kitchen. He took the view that any meal he could not prepare inside ten minutes was not a serious option. He toasted two slices of wholemeal to have with the salmon and opened a bottle of Australian red, not for his stomach's sake but in the hope that it might stimulate his weary mind. He preferred red with smoked fish, and anyway he enjoyed kicking over the traces of suburban convention in memory of his countryman father.

He felt out of sorts, mainly because of Anna and the proprietorial interest she was taking in his work. He was not in her pay. He was his own man. He must make her see that the book was his and his alone. On the other hand, he would have to keep her happy; he needed access to all the source materials in her possession, and he was by no means convinced that she had shown him everything. Quite possibly, she knew of the existence of Maguire's *journal intime*; and if she did, how could he convince her to let him read it? It was a job for a diplomat rather than a journalist, someone with her late husband's skills in the black arts of persuasion.

When he had eaten, he poured himself another glass of wine and took from his jacket pocket the precious moleskin diary. The pages were unlined, and the handwriting small. As a narrative it was perfectly intelligible, apart from what he could only describe as printer's marks such as daggers, double daggers, braces and carets. Did they mean something, or were they Maguire's idea of a posthumous joke? The most common mark was 'L', which could have referred to paragraphing or indeed to Louise Lamotte. Sometimes 'L' was preceded by 'J', and sometimes 'J' by 'L'. Whenever these signs occurred, they were followed by a dagger, double dagger or a caret mark. Assuming the 'L' stood for Louise and 'J' for Jim, the printer's marks that followed might conceivably have a sexual significance. He would have to begin at the beginning and work his way through the diary page by page in the hope that some shaft of light might fall. He would have to compare 'JL§', 'LJ†', 'JL‡' and 'LJƒ', and work out what on earth they might mean.

The very first sentence was a generalisation, which invited immediate concurrence or dissent:

Every man has his own private Avernus, which he enters again and again in the hope of finding Elysium. When I look across the chamber at the blank faces of the opposition, I think of L's bare buttocks rising to greet me. On bad days I think of the Cyclops; on good days I yearn for Elysium. But Elysium is a dream that on waking turns to Hades, a land of cold and shadow, a chamber in which the white faces of the opposition smirk in the gloom.

The diary was a curious mixture of self-analysis, self-pity and self-flagellation.

I grow old, I grow old. Loss of hair, ambition, virility. I am on a fast-moving treadmill, and I can't get off. Anna finds fulfilment among her fairies, L gives me four out of ten, and Sarah puts out a new rumour every day. Even Bishop's Delight has lost all savour— apples on the Dead Sea shore, all ashes to the taste. Thank heavens for MacBride; he's the only man I can trust. My oldest friend is Woody. A humble wordsmith, my weathercock and weatherglass. From his questions I can tell what the unfortunate taxpayers are thinking. Taxpayers are my paymasters; they dice with my future, and Woody and his like feed them their only pabulum on a spoon. I depend on journalists; they span the gulf between me and the man in the drain. I talk to them all, but I pay Woody in extra nods and winks, which more often than not he converts into scoops. Like me, he's no saint. He will remain my friend while I pay him in convertible currency. I often wonder if I should take him more fully into my confidence. After all, he probably thinks the world of me. Many famous men had friends on whom they could depend, Montaigne and King David among them. I wouldn't go so far as to wish Woody were my Jonathan, but I owe him a debt of gratitude—when I filched Anna from under his nose, he took it on the chin like a man. Give me a man who knows the limits of his worth and I'll take him any day for a friend.

He was touched by Maguire's good opinion of him, but he did not like the reference to his ready acceptance of the loss of Anna. He had never accepted the loss of her, and he took a dim view of Maguire's idea of friendship. He was forever quoting his literary hero Montaigne, but in his cynicism he was closer to La Rochefoucauld. Maguire did not know himself. His diary was but a half-hearted attempt at self-scrutiny. In climbing so high, he had exposed his arse for all to see, while remaining blithely oblivious of those looking up from below.

He went back over what he'd just read, pausing to wonder what Bishop's Delight might be. He thought of Turkish delight, and concluded that Bishop's Delight was a dessert once favoured in ecclesiastical circles. But why describe it as a Dead Sea fruit? Several pages further on he came upon an entry that suggested a possible answer:

The end of a perfect little divertimento, I fear. I always make sure that the coast is clear before ringing L's doorbell. This evening as I pretended to look in the window of the shop opposite, I thought I saw a figure emerge from her street door whose hat and turned-up collar reminded me of Humphrey Bogart playing Philip Marlowe. I froze as I saw the face. Beyond doubt, that aquiline nose and out-thrust chin belonged to one of our most powerful bishops, noted in particular for the astringency of his pastoral letters and his inquisitorial skills in the confessional. Rather shaken, I climbed the stairs to find L in her floral negligee, smoking a cigarette and eating honey from a spoon.

'You've just had a visit from His Excellency, I see.'

'He's very sweet. He always brings me a comb of honey. His brother, God bless him, keeps bees.'

'So there's honey for tea whenever he drops in?'

'Now you're putting bad thoughts in my head,' she smiled.

'What's his predilection, then?'

'Bishop's Delight of course.'

'I hope he gives you absolution as well as honey?'

She laughed as she unbuttoned, and asked if I'd like her to taste sweet.

Regretfully, I must give up seeing her. It has become too risky. I keep imagining the brouhaha should it come to light that a beleaguered Taoiseach and the most outspoken bishop in the country share the affections of a lingerie model. So what must I do then? Where should I go? Paris? Amsterdam? Tahiti? Sadly, the Manao tupapau girl is dead by now. All Leinster House and no Bishop's Delight is a recipe for abject misery.

The last entry in the diary was particularly interesting:

My coalition partners are growing restive, threatening to withdraw their support if I don't call an election in the autumn. The house is falling. The beaten men come into their own. Oh, for a comfortable majority! Democracy at its best posits the idea of an educated and discerning electorate, a public that makes the interests of the country its own. Even the paid hacks are contemptuous. They say quite openly that we Irish are deficient in civic morality and that there is no hope for Ireland while we connive at dishonesty and dishonour in public life. Someone else said, 'Politicians and nappies need changing regularly, and for similar reasons.' Our honey-bearing bishop would undoubtedly agree.

He had no idea why the diary should end three weeks before Maguire's disappearance. The notebook could not conceivably have been an isolated burst of self-exposure. More than likely, it was part of a sequence. But where were the others? And, more important, was Anna aware of them? If so, what on earth had she made of them?'

The notebook raised certain questions, to which Louise Lamotte might well have the answers. If nothing else, she would know about Bishop's Delight, a possibility that threatened to inflame his imagination. Reluctant though he was to turn a dangerous corner, he would have to get in touch with her again. He would have to feign an interest in her pathetic kiss-and-tell book, of course, but it was all in the worthy cause of discovering what Maguire had been up to.

While Sweetman would go on piously about the public interest and the public's right to know, he himself was a lone star ranger. He was in journalism to earn a living, and his only resources were his loathing of pretence, his sense of isolation and injured merit, and his desire to uncover the pure and unadulterated truth, not for the so-called public good but simply for his own gratification.

16

They had finished eating, and Kevin had poured what was left of the wine, holding the bottle ceremoniously over his glass for the last drip. Jane was in talkative mood. She had been to the hairdresser's that morning, and he had noticed her new coiffure without having to be prompted, which pleased her no end. If nothing else, it showed that he paid attention to how she looked and noticed things that had nothing to do with bonking.

'We'll go to bed now,' he said, draining his glass.

'No, we won't. We'll watch the news first.'

'Nothing ever happens at weekends. Besides, the news reminds me of work. The weekend is my time to be with you.'

'You hypocrite! It's just as well I know better than to believe you.'

She got up and, taking his hand, led him into the living room. Having given him a lingering kiss to be going on with, she switched on the television. The news was already in progress, and Sweetman was interviewing a middle-aged lady of stern diction and formidable bearing.

'Let me get this straight,' Sweetman was saying. 'Where were you standing at the time?'

'On the pavement opposite the entrance to the Musée d'Orsay,' she replied.

'Now this is very important. Tell me precisely what you saw.'

'I saw a tall, lean man coming out. At first I couldn't believe that I was looking at Jim Maguire. He had dyed his hair white; it was his thick black eyebrows that gave him away. He hasn't changed a bit—still the same straight-backed strut and the same well-cut suit. At first I thought I was seeing things, but when I saw a big, burly man coming out after him I knew I had seen something I wasn't meant to see. I followed them along the river for a hundred yards, then they both got into a taxi and that was the last I saw of them. I think they may have realised that they'd been spotted.'

'And who was the big, burly man?'

'Bill MacBride, of course. I recognised him at once.'

'Is there any possibility you might have been mistaken?'

'None. I live near Phoenix Park. I've often seen them both out jogging together as I walked my dogs.'

'So you're not in any doubt?'

'None whatever.'

'That was Sadie McGowan who has just returned from a week in Paris. Her story is interesting. If nothing else, it cries out to be investigated.'

'Another nutcase!' Jane said. 'We'll never hear the end of Maguire and MacBride.'

'It could be a red herring, but it's just possible there's something in it.'

'We'll have a rest now,' she said. 'It will put the news in perspective.'

'I need to make a few quick phone calls first.'

'No, you don't. You said the weekend was to be mine.' She took him by the hand and smiled up at him. 'Now, get them off you! Isn't that what you always say to me?'

They started undressing, one on either side of the bed. Woody was first in. He lay on his back, listening to the rustling. 'No, don't take off your bra and knickers! There's nothing like a few flimsy obstacles to stimulate the old endorphins.'

'And who are they when they're at home?'

'I haven't the foggiest. I was only trying to impress you.'

'Now, no charging or rushing, and no storming the gates. Maguire and MacBride can wait. They'll still be living it up in Paris tomorrow.'

Resolving to get the better of her for once, he spent the best part of an hour in foreplay. He had almost exhausted his considerable repertoire when she finally gave the signal to lower the drawbridge. They were ravening and ravenous; they went for the kill like hawks. Sated, they fell asleep in each other's arms. It was ten minutes past three when he woke to find that she was still by his side. It was the first time she had stayed the night. He was in uncharted territory. As he lay wondering what to do next, she turned on her side and put her hand down inside his pyjamas.

'I feel very rested,' she said. 'I'll never get back to sleep now without a sedative. What do you prescribe?'

'I've got some Mogadon in the bathroom.'

'I'd rather something that doesn't cause morning drowsiness.' She gave his erect penis a little tug.

Within minutes he found himself engaging her in single combat again, while his mind ran on likely headlines in the morning papers. Ransacking his vocabulary for English words that rhymed with Musée d'Orsay, the best he could do was 'Sexual Horseplay'. It wasn't good enough. Sweetman, he felt sure, would do better. Too much excitement was sapping his imagination. If married life was anything like this, he'd never get a wink of sleep or time to finish his biography. 'I'm sure to drop off now,' she said finally. He waited patiently for five or ten minutes, then stole downstairs to make himself a cheese and pickle sandwich, which he washed down with a glass of elderflower cordial.

When he got back to bed, she was snoring softly. He lay on his back, trying to anticipate every conceivable variation on the Musée d'Orsay story. He was aware of Jane lying by his side; the heat from her body gave him a sense of comfort that was new to him. But all that was by the way. He felt saddened by the latest twist in the Maguire–MacBride story: it was too banal, a gift to the tabloids and all journalists who gloried in defamatory innuendo. It played into Sweetman's hands, and made his own chosen course harder to follow.

He must have slept. She was shaking him by the shoulder when he opened his eyes.

'I thought I'd pamper you for once,' she said. 'I've brought you breakfast.'

She had placed the tray on the night table: half a grapefruit, a boiled egg, two slices of buttered toast and coffee. He looked at his watch; it was six thirty-five. He would listen to the seven o'clock news.

'I'll be going now,' she said. 'Believe it or not, I have to get to work.'

'You shouldn't have gone to all this trouble.'

'It was no trouble. It was the best weekend we've ever had.' She kissed him on the cheek. 'You'd better shave,' she said. 'Your chin is a rasp.'

She blew him another kiss from the doorway and was gone. He felt relieved to be alone again. He didn't mind being pampered in bed on occasion, but he didn't like the idea of unpredictable pampering. He'd always cooked his own breakfast, except on holiday when he ordered from the menu. This morning he'd fancied two bacon rashers and an egg with two slices of black pudding and a fried tomato. But she wasn't to know that, so he could hardly blame her. She was a little gem. She made him feel guilty; she was so sincere in everything she said and did.

He himself lived in a world of mirrors and distorted images that could not be put in writing without further distortion. It was strange for him to come back to Jane's truth-telling, which struck him at times as an implicit criticism of the life he had chosen to lead. She was no comforter; she said what she thought without editing a word of it, even at the risk of offending him. In moments of self-criticism he thought of her as the only genuine person in his life.

Tapping his egg and topping it gave him a little lift. It was just right, neither too hard nor too runny, and the coffee was good and strong. He'd left the grapefruit till last because that was his fancy this morning. It wasn't something he could have done in Jane's company without inviting comment. It was one of the advantages of the bachelor life as he saw it, being free to please oneself in every particular, to live one's life without having to take account of well-meant criticism or advice. Solitude was important, especially for a man who spent most of his time in company he did not greatly value. On the other hand, he was fond of Jane. He liked her sense of humour, which was not the humour of other women. She grew up as the only girl in a family of seven. She knew how to hold her own among men. She saw them as an interesting variation on her own thoughts and feelings, and she preferred their conversation to that of her own sex. She'd told him more than once that the difference between men and women was greatly exaggerated because it was in the interest of some easily identified women to stir up trouble.

In many ways, Jane was the most original woman he'd ever met. Her only fault was her desire to make him look like a banker—wanting to make him dress less shabbily and to do something about his unruly hair—things that weren't matters of high principle, but could become the thin end of a very thick wedge. There was no need to worry, though. He wouldn't take a leap in the dark. He'd always found that situations left simmering long enough finally resolve themselves.

He switched on the radio for the news. There was an interview with the police superintendent whose team was investigating the disappearance of Maguire and MacBride, but nothing new had come to light. When he had washed and shaved, he phoned Sweetman to ask how much significance he attached to Sadie McGowan's story. Sweetman was devious, of course. He didn't expect him to say what he really thought, but he might unwittingly drop a hint that would point the way to an unexplored angle.

'I watched your interview with Sadie McGowan,' he said. 'A red herring, if ever there was one.'

'Don't be so sure. Sadie's no crank. She can tell what's news from what isn't.'

'How much did you have to pay her?'

'Not a cent. I just bought her a drink and listened to what she had to say. In case you're interested, her tipple is kir royale.'

'She may be good for a paragraph in a longer piece. But it's probably too late. Her story is already dead.'

'Wrong again, Woody. It's only the first chapter. It will run and run. I'll make sure of that.'

'How is your Parisian courtesan these days?'

'She's on the case while on the job. She's in touch with every high-class hooker in Paris. Sooner or later, Mag and Mac will fancy a bit of the other. As soon as they do, I'll be on their tail. You don't play hide-and-seek with Tony Sweetman.'

'Anything else in the offing?'

'There's a big story about to break, but my lips are sealed till one o'clock. Watch the lunchtime news.'

'I think I know. Maguire's favourite fantasy was sex with a ballerina in her tutu. One of his victims has finally decided to tell us what it was like.'

'Now there's a story! The image it conjures up out-tutus anything by Degas. Would you like me to make it come true?'

Sweetman thought he was being clever, but unwittingly he'd given him a fresh angle. He would get in touch with Sadie McGowan and write a piece about her holiday in Paris. He would give an unvarnished report of what she did and thought, indirectly revealing the kind of windbag she was and thereby undermining her credibility. It would also show up Sweetman's account of her story as a piece of overheated piffle.

He was about to get in touch with Anna when Louise phoned. 'Have you heard the latest?' she breathed excitedly. 'It's all over the papers. Maguire and MacBride have been spotted in Paris. Anything that keeps the public guessing is good for my book.'

'That's yesterday's news,' he said. 'For the latest, you must listen in at lunchtime.'

'So what is the latest?'

'My lips are sealed till one o'clock, I'm afraid.'

'I've got something to show you. I thought nothing of it at the time, but it could be worth a small fortune now.'

'I'm up to my neck in work, Louise, and I've got a meeting at twelve-thirty.'

'This won't take long. It's a real eye-opener.'

'What can it be?'

'Photos of you-know-who *in flagrante*. Isn't that how you say it?'

'I'll see you in about half an hour.'

He knew he shouldn't. The memory of her kiss still disturbed him. He kept thinking of it even while he was with Jane. He arrived on her doorstep at eleven. She'd already done her hair, but she was still in her floral negligee, smelling of bath oil and synthetic sweetness. In clicking high heels she led him to her sofa, and they both sat down. He watched as she took a bundle of photos from an envelope and laid them out before him on the coffee table. They showed the naked bodies of a man and woman making love in various contorted positions. He examined them one by one to make sure it was the same male body throughout.

'How did you ever manage to take these?'

'That's my little secret. One day I'll tell you, but not yet. How much are they worth?'

'They'd be worth a lot if they showed heads as well as buttocks and genitals.'

'It's obviously the body of a tall, thin man, and the woman is me, as you can see.' She opened her negligee to let him have a good look at her figure.

'I'm not disputing that. The headless man could even be me, or any other man with a light physique like Maguire's.'

'But it isn't you or any other man. It's Maguire, I'm telling you. And it didn't just end there. I'll show you my instruments of torture now that you're here.'

'Surely Maguire wasn't a masochist as well?'

'Only on rare occasions. Sometimes after a punishing day at Leinster House. He used to say it was homeopathic. But what really got him going was a touch of what he called Bishop's Delight.'

'Never heard of it.'

'I can't describe what it meant to him in words, but some time when you're not in such a desperate hurry I'll show you. It's one of those things you must experience for yourself. You may be able to describe it; I haven't got the words, I'm afraid.'

'We'll have to describe it in the book,' he said. 'I can't write about it unless I know what it is.'

'We'll just call it my speciality.'

'Come on, give us a clue, Louise,' he smiled.

'Don't be a naughty boy now.' She tweaked his nose. 'Instead, I'll give you a little kiss to be going on with.'

It was a long kiss that sent an electrical charge down his spine and legs. His head swam; he felt quite faint. Worse still, he couldn't get to his feet without betraying his all-too-obvious condition.

'Maguire used to call me his little kinkajou.' She laughed and pressed her thigh against his.

'His kinkajou?'

'Apparently it can suck nectar from flowers with its tongue.'

'You learn something new every day.' He felt relieved. The thought of a kinkajou's tongue in his mouth had brought him back to earth. Thankfully, it was now safe to get up.

'When are you going to make a start on my book?'

'First you must do an outline, then I'll know where we're going. I need to know the beginning, the middle and the end. Can you do that for next Monday?'

'You've given me an imposition. It's like being back in the convent.'

'Don't worry, it isn't an essay. Just make a list of all the things you want to include as they happen to occur to you. I'll put them in the right order.'

'Will you do something for me before you go? Will you massage my tummy? I've got a terrible pain here.'

She unbuttoned her negligee and lay out invitingly on the sofa with one foot on the floor. He knelt down and spent a pleasant five or ten minutes helping to relieve whatever was troubling her.

'Don't be shy,' she said. 'You can put your hand where the pain is, down inside my panties.'

'Are you sure it isn't something serious? Maybe you should see a doctor.'

'You're better than any doctor I know. Your touch is so soothing, Kevin.'

After a while she said, 'Oh, what a relief! It's gone. It must have been trapped wind.'

He felt pleased to have made his escape without need for further palpation. He was beginning to understand the deep, dark waters he had ventured into. As he cycled home, he kept asking himself, 'What would Jane think?' He sensed that somehow he had betrayed her. Though he hadn't done anything wrong, he had done something he couldn't tell her about. It was all part of his job, of course, but Jane was the kind of girl who simply wouldn't understand.

17

His twelve-thirty meeting was a fiction, an excuse to escape from what he saw coming only too clearly. He owed Jane an allegiance he'd never owed any other woman. He knew that he must not go to bed with Louise, but no matter how hard he pedalled, he couldn't put the memory of her kiss behind him. She was prettier than Jane, and she gave him an erection from merely thinking about her. Unlike Jane, though, she wasn't original. She never said anything that surprised him; her whole conversation was about Louise and the wonderful theatrical future she had planned for herself. And the stage was only the beginning, she'd said: what she really dreamed of was a life on film. She could then go to the cinema and see herself as other people saw her.

'I'll be leading two lives simultaneously. We're all only here for a jiffy. To tap every vein you've got, you need to lead a thousand lives in one. No, not a thousand but a hundred thousand, because I'll live in the imagination of everyone who sees me on the screen. Young men will dream about me and compare their girlfriends' faces with mine. Can you imagine it? Even thinking about it makes me dizzy.'

He had caught himself out. In spite of his best efforts he was still thinking about her. In an effort to escape from her magnetic field, he directed his attention to what was all round him: horn-hooting motorists, impatient pedestrians, a policeman looking as if he'd seen it all too often before. Dublin had changed since his boyhood. One day he would write a book called *Where Has Dear Old Dublin Gone?* mourning the death of the pubs, shops and public buildings of his youth. Practically all that remained of the old O'Connell Street was Daniel O'Connell himself. Countless generations of seagulls had splattered and whitened his noble head, but still he stood obdurately on his plinth facing south-west, facing the real Ireland, his own Ireland, the Ireland of the rural poor who paid him in pennies they could ill afford. What would he have made of the frivolities of the Celtic Tiger if he'd glimpsed them fleetingly in a dream?

He watched the one o'clock news. Sweetman had put on a solemn face in keeping with the gravity of the words on his autocue. The bank of which MacBride was a director was in financial difficulty. Already customers were queuing to withdraw their savings, and the acting Taoiseach would be making a statement in an hour's time. Furthermore, there had been suggestions that MacBride had paid substantial sums of money into Maguire's account, and the leader of the opposition had tabled a motion demanding a public inquiry into possible wrongdoing.

'Sex is dead for now,' his editor said when he phoned. 'This is about money. Write me a piece from the point of view of the little man with all his savings in one bank. Try to answer the question "Where will it end?" leaving eschatology out of it. This is the most serious thing that's happened in living memory. We must give it all we've got.'

He phoned Anna to tell her that he wouldn't be able to come that afternoon. She hadn't listened to the lunchtime news, and she seemed slow to take in what he told her. 'I said I'd cook dinner for you. I'm roasting a leg of lamb. Surely you don't expect me to eat it all by myself?'

'I'll try to be with you by seven,' he said. 'I'm having one of those days.'

'I'll expect you to carve, so don't be late.'

He cycled downtown to see what was going on and to interview one or two of the editor's 'little men'. For good measure he talked to four or five big women and one or two teenagers as well. The enormity of the news hadn't quite sunk in. The men said they weren't in the least surprised; all of them blamed Maguire and MacBride. The women, who were more practical, said they would be taking no chances with their savings. He phoned the professor of economics at Trinity to get what his editor called 'the big picture'. Then he went home to deliver himself of the wise words that had been burgeoning all afternoon somewhere at the back of his mind. It was six by the time he'd filed his piece, and by then it was time to think of Anna.

As soon as she opened the door, he could tell that she had been drinking. At times she could be rather distant. Today, she was all over him. She offered him her cheek for a kiss, a rare honour, and led him into the living room, where she gave him a gin and tonic in a tall glass, which was so stiff that he felt constrained to ask for more tonic.

'I've had a challenging afternoon,' she said. 'I'm writing a fairy tale in modern dress, since children don't believe in real fairies any more. It's curious how stories never change. There are only a limited number of fairy stories you can tell. All that changes from country to country and from century to century are the actors and their trappings. The stories remain the same.'

'In journalism everything can be reduced to either sex or money. But it's worse in fairy tales, I imagine. They all must have a happy ending. The sameness of it would defeat me utterly.'

'On the contrary, it's a challenge. A good storyteller has a thousand arrows in her quiver. She can make the old as new as the sunrise every morning.'

He felt weary after his literary efforts, and the thought of a woman with a thousand arrows in her quiver was too much for his romantic soul. He was about to sink down into Anna's beckoning sofa when she said, 'Now we'll eat. All is ready. It's a simple hors d'oeuvre: prosciutto and avocado. You needn't worry; I bought four avocados to make sure I got one that was eatable.'

He tried to interest her in the bank news, but she was still obsessed with fairy tales; she would talk of nothing else.

'For the past ten years we've been living a fairy tale here in Ireland. The evidence is all around us in the streets and in the shops.'

He tried to bring her down to earth. 'For some artists an unhappy childhood provides a magic fountain they keep revisiting for refreshment throughout their lives.'

She ignored his comment. 'My childhood was happy and my subsequent life unhappy. That's my personal tragedy. I write fairy tales because they provide opportunities for cruelty that stops short of total disaster.'

He could see that she was quite drunk. She wasn't slurring her words, but her thinking made no sense to him whatever. It was the thinking of a pampered woman who'd never had to worry about either cost or value. He felt impatient; he kept wondering what Jane would say about her self-indulgent maunderings.

The lamb was not only roasted but frazzled, which, happily, was how he liked lamb. He couldn't understand the craze in modern restaurants for rare lamb, what he called Frenchified lamb. Anna's lamb might not carve very elegantly, but it tasted delicious, and the bottle of Pomerol she provided as an accompaniment was a vast improvement on his Sunday supermarket claret.

'I know that Jim has been criticised for giving the Irish people a ten-year spree without thought for the ultimate cost,' she said. 'His critics say he did it to ensure he remained in office, but irresponsibility in politics was the least of his faults.'

'He was a complex man. He wasn't easy to get to know. I thought I knew him at university and later at the magazine, but once he entered parliament he took colour from the people round him.' He was trying to get her to talk about Jim, and he wondered if perhaps he'd gone too far.

'He put on a public mask like the rest of them,' she said. 'The problem with a mask is if you wear it for long enough, the face underneath becomes the mask. Finally, there's no need for the mask. The public man eats the private man until nothing remains but the outer shell.'

'Do you think that happened to Jim?'

'I know it did. The man I found myself living with in recent years was not the man I married. I've been very unhappy, Kevin. I never told anyone before.'

Now he was worried that she might let slip something she'd regret in the sober light of morning. 'We've all known periods of unhappiness,' he said. 'We wouldn't be ourselves without them.'

'I wouldn't have minded the buffetings of fate. The unhappiness in my life came from Jim's repeated infidelities. That's something I can neither understand nor forgive. And it was so unnecessary. It wasn't as if I were a prudish Victorian matron.'

Why was she telling him all this? It wasn't like her to let conversation veer into dangerous waters. He did not wish to know the intimate details of their bedroom, but he felt helpless to change the subject.

'Jim was an old fraud. The man you all thought you knew wasn't the real man at all. From start to finish, his life was a lie,' she continued.

He could not imagine what had got into her. She'd always been so circumspect in her comments, so careful to protect Jim's reputation and legacy. Surely it couldn't all be put down to a swig too many.

'All politicians live a lie,' he said. 'They have to, because the public will always vote for the comforting illusion rather than the harsh and warty truth. It's human nature. We're all in the lie together.'

'We mustn't put all the blame on the public. Jim was better at lying than most. He once told me that the only reason he still remained in office after three elections was that he could distinguish between what the public will believe from what it will not. That, I think, puts a different complexion on your theory.'

She reached for the wine bottle and topped up her glass, which was already half full. Then she took a 'sip' that reduced the contents by half.

'For dessert we're having one of my special sherry trifles made with muffins, black cherries, mascarpone and crème fraiche. You'll find it on the worktop in the kitchen, and you'll find the dishes on the sideboard there behind you.'

Wondering if she saw him as her butler for the evening, he went into the kitchen, which was a reassuring picture of domestic chaos that reminded him of home. A pile of unwashed plates filled the sink, and greasy pots and pans disfigured the ultra-modern worktop. The dessert bowl was on the breakfast table in the centre of the room, looking the more inviting for the disorder that surrounded it. Ceremoniously, he bore the bowl into the dining room, only to find her fast asleep at the table. She had pushed back her plate and rested her folded arms and head on the table mat. Her dry grey hair looked unkempt. She was the same age as him, yet she looked ten years older. For a moment he stood helplessly with the dessert bowl between his hands, at a loss about what to do.

'Anna,' he said, 'would you like me to spoon out the trifle?' He placed the bowl on the table, but she neither moved nor raised her head.

He carried the dirty plates out to the kitchen and put them on top of the pile in the sink. He got two dessert dishes from the sideboard and placed them beside the dessert bowl on the table. Then he laid his hand lightly on her shoulder and shook it. She raised her head and looked around the room as if in alarm.

'You've been away a long time,' she said. 'What have you been doing?'

'Getting the trifle from the kitchen.'

'Is that all? I'm so tired; I must have slept. I wrote five hundred words today, which means I had to write three thousand. How many did you write?'

'Two thousand.'

'But how many did you have to write to get two thousand?'

'About two thousand two hundred.'

'You must be very efficient, or maybe not so very choosy. Which is it?'

'I'm not a perfectionist. No journalist can afford to be.'

'I can't keep my eyes open. Will you help me up the stairs?'

'Don't you want some dessert?'

'I'll have it in bed. And I'll have coffee too. I'm stuck to this chair. Maybe you could dislodge me.'

He put a hand under each arm and helped her out of her chair. Then he put an arm around her waist and they climbed the dogleg stairs, step by careful step. When he'd put her sitting in the armchair in her bedroom, she told him that she would get ready for bed while he had his dessert and made the coffee. He would find an open bottle of malmsey in the kitchen to have with the trifle if that was what he fancied; and he would find a bottle of Highland Park on the dining room sideboard if he wished for a little *digestif.*

Her trifle was excellent. He resisted the lure of the malmsey and instead poured himself a fine shot of the Highland Park to keep him company while he made the coffee. He was beginning to enjoy his buttling, taking perverse delight in the contemplation of his new role as he imagined she must see it. What he couldn't understand was the change in her attitude to Jim. The last time he'd spoken to her she wouldn't hear a wrong word said against him; now she was among his most trenchant critics. She had said things that not even Sweetman would risk saying in public. He wouldn't press her further this evening; he would wait and see what she said on his next visit, and he would make sure to come in the morning while her mind was still fresh.

He found her sitting up in bed reading. She had combed her hair and put on her glasses. She looked transformed, the very picture of matronly respectability.

'That little snooze did me good,' she said. 'Now if I drop off, it won't matter. Make sure you wait to hear the click of the latch as you let yourself out.'

'What are you reading?' he asked.

'*The Wind in the Willows*, a book I would recommend to all aspirant politicians and political journalists. I kept pressing it on Jim, but he told me not to be silly. He just couldn't see it as a manual of political life. He himself was the living counterpart of Badger, solitary and sensible, a born leader and a courageous fighter. When I told him so, he said that I should try something more becoming like Montaigne's essays. We all dig our own graves.'

When she'd dispatched the trifle and the coffee, she asked him to bring up the Highland Park. 'We'll have a little tincture and talk about the book,' she said.

He took her at her word and poured her a 'tincture', but she promptly told him not to be so niggardly and insisted that he treat himself equally generously. Then she asked him to draw up the armchair so that she could look at him without having to crick her neck.

'I won't beat about the bush,' she said. 'We've had ten years of deception and dishonesty. So why write a work of hagiography? We'll paint Jim as he was, warts and all.'

For a moment he didn't know what to say. He suspected some kind of trap. He looked down into the amber liquor in his glass, as if trying to divine the future of his magnum opus.

'What made you change your mind?' he asked.

'You did. You said you wanted to write a book as a counterbalance to Sweetman's. We'll go one better: we'll write a book to overbalance his. We'll let it all hang out. Isn't that what they say these days?'

'Sweetman has a team of researchers at his disposal. We're at a disadvantage there.'

'No, we're not. I have all the documents you need here in this house, copies of papers, minutes of meetings, personal diaries, the lot. All strong stuff. The problem will be watering down, not flowering up.'

'What I've seen of the journal isn't encouraging,' he said.

'You haven't seen his sex diaries. As they stand, they're not fit for the eye of the common reader. We'll have to water them down in the interest of public morality.'

She was obviously referring to the missing moleskin diaries. He couldn't wait to get his hands on them. They would bring much-needed yeast to the glutinous dough and make his biography a commercial as well as a critical success. She had closed her eyes. He wondered if she had fallen asleep again. He felt desperately tired, but still curious to hear what she might come out with next. He drained his glass and closed his eyes.

'Kevin!' she said, 'you're not falling asleep on me, are you?'

'No, I'm just resting my eyes from the light.'

'Here, take my hand. I've done you a terrible injustice, and I'm sorry. I was taken in by appearances and grand words. Can you ever forgive me for my stupidity?'

'There's nothing to forgive. You're one of my oldest friends, and I hope you see me in the same light.'

'You loved me once and I let you down. The hurt I caused you is still on my mind.'

'It was a long time ago, Anna. We're both different people now. The important thing is that we're still friends.'

'I'm pleased to hear it. Kiss me to show there's no ill feeling.'

He kissed her on the cheek, and she closed her eyes and smiled. 'Now hold my hand until I drop off. When I do, you can kiss me good night and let yourself out.'

He held her hand and closed his eyes. When he opened them again, he felt stiff in his limbs. The light was still on and Anna was facing the wall, fast asleep. The bottle of Highland Park was empty, his tongue tasted of sand, and his skull was threatening to split in two. Worse still, it was almost five-thirty by his watch.

He stole down the stairs and let himself out. He cycled down the driveway into the indifferent street. Rain was falling softly from an overcast sky as the glistening tarmac vanished beneath him. The houses on each side looked thin as theatre props; there was no traffic and no one about. He felt that in someone else's past he had seen it all before. Then it came to him, the lines from *In Memoriam*:

> *And ghastly through the drizzling rain*
> *On the bald street breaks the blank day.*

As he neared home he passed a lost soul wandering aimlessly, as if in a fog. He was surprised to find the light on in the hallway, and shocked to find Jane having breakfast in the kitchen.

'Where on earth have you been?' she asked.

'I had dinner with Anna last night. She wasn't feeling well. I just couldn't leave her all on her own.'

'It's a good one. You should tell it to the marines.'

'It happens to be true. She lives on her own. If anything happened to her, I'd never be able to forgive myself.'

'What's between you and Mrs Maguire?'

'I'm writing her late husband's biography. She has all the documents I need for the job.'

'So that's it. You spent the night on the job.'

'Jane! How can you say such a thing?'

'Mammy's been told she has terminal cancer. I didn't want to tell you over the phone, so I came around after dinner thinking you'd be here. I waited and waited. Then it was too late to go home, so I slept on your sofa for the first and last time.'

'Jane, listen to me. I can explain everything. Anna is an old friend. She's elderly. There's nothing between us, I can assure you.'

'You love words. Surely you must know that the empty ones make most sound. Goodbye, Kevin. Here's your door key. I won't be needing it again.'

Leaving her half-eaten breakfast on the table, she picked up her handbag and made for the door. She was being unreasonable, of course, but he blamed himself for having given her a door key. He wouldn't have done so if she hadn't given him a key to her flat. Now he would have to waste valuable time making her see sense again. He was sorry to hear about her mother. She was close to Jane as the only girl in the family. Still, there was nothing he could do. He would just have to give her time to simmer down. Twenty-four hours of heart-searching should do the trick. He would invite her out to dinner. There was no point in trying to get her to admit that she was wrong because, like political journalism, this wasn't about the truth. For an easy life he would have to put on a long face, appear in sackcloth and ashes, and say that he was heartily sorry for his sins. He had fallen for her because she was different. If 'different' meant 'headstrong and unpredictable', he would have to live with it. Ultimately, he had no one to blame but himself.

18

MacBride was discovered on the smallest of the Aran Islands, Innisheer, staying with an old couple, living quietly and going for walks on the cliffs every day. He had told them that he was resting after a long illness, that he had lost his wife and was alone in the world. He'd had a dog called Slipper once, but even his dog had deserted him. All he wished for now was to live quietly until he regained his strength.

The doctor who examined him said that he was suffering from amnesia, and that all he could remember was the name of his lost spaniel. He was brought back to Dublin from Galway in an ambulance for examination by his private doctor, who said that his patient was in 'fugue state', a mental condition probably brought on by stress or worry. This was a classic case of psychogenic amnesia, he said, and it was typical of such patients to try to put physical distance between themselves and whatever had caused their distress. It was a temporary condition that normally responded to treatment. After recovery, previous memories would return almost intact.

Woody had expected Sweetman to eat humble pie, since he'd claimed both on television and in print that MacBride had gone to Paris to enjoy the fleshpots with his friend Maguire. Sweetman, however, was unrepentant. He interviewed several pensioners who had invested their life savings in 'MacBride's bank', and he wondered if MacBride's amnesia might have been assumed in order to attract public sympathy. If he was so forgetful, why had he put most of his personal assets, including four substantial villas, in his wife's name? It was interesting to note that his friend Maguire had put all his property and most of his investments in his wife's name as well. One of the pensioners he interviewed wished that he could afford to employ the brilliant accountants who regulated MacBride and Maguire's affairs. Sweetman then told him that the services of brilliant accountants were 'the preserve of the stinking rich, and not for the likes of you and me'. The pensioner agreed that there was no justice for the small man; justice was strictly for those who could pay the exorbitant price. It made good television, even though everyone knew that Sweetman had coached his pensioners in what to say and how to say it.

Woody felt that he should stay out of the fray until MacBride had made a full recovery. He wished to interview him again about Maguire, and he knew better than to queer his pitch in the meantime. Instead he talked to a doctor and a psychiatrist and confined himself to a discussion of MacBride's medical condition, the likely causes, and the expected period of recuperation. No one would describe his article as 'sensationalist', but his editor was pleased by the number of letters it inspired, describing readers' personal experience of temporary memory loss, which, it would seem, was not uncommon.

No matter where he turned, the question of what to do about Louise and her photographs haunted him. He was reluctant to get involved, but he felt he must see her to tell her finally that he was too busy to ghost her book. At a pinch he could fit it in, of course, but it was far too risky given Jane's sensitivity to other women. If she took exception to Anna, what would she make of Louise? He was about to press Louise's buzzer, when the door opened and one of the other tenants came out. He climbed the stairs with his head down, thinking of what he should say to her. He was stopped in his tracks by a familiar voice from the landing above.

'One out; one in. It's like confessions.' Sweetman gave him his most superior smile.

'She isn't expecting me. I'm just dropping by for a chat.'

'I hadn't realised we shared an *amoureuse*.'

'Louise has nothing to do with my love life. I've known her since she was a schoolgirl.'

'Lucky you to have known her in spring time. We're men of the world, Woody. We must compare notes. I'm dying to have your thoughts on Bishop's Delight. Lunchtime Friday perhaps?'

'Neary's at twelve then.'

He lingered on the landing until Sweetman had gone. He was shocked. It hadn't occurred to him that Sweetman might know her. Now he could understand Maguire's horror when he saw a certain bishop emerge from her door. It was all becoming far too complicated, and to compound matters, Sweetman knew about Bishop's Delight. It was all too much; he simply couldn't face Louise again. He would phone and tell her that he was up to his neck in work and couldn't help out. She wouldn't give it a second thought. She would turn to Sweetman or someone else; she probably knew every lecherous hack in town. Quietly, he descended the stairs and let himself out.

As soon as he got home, he phoned her. She listened in silence until he had finished.

'I don't understand,' she said. 'Last time we met you seemed enthusiastic. Was it something I said?'

'Of course not. It's just the sheer pressure of work.'

'Was it something you heard? If it was, I'd like to know.'

'It's none of those things, believe me. I'm just too busy to give your book the time and attention it deserves.'

'I'm disappointed. I thought I could help you while you helped me.'

'I'm sorry, Louise.'

'Could you come around tomorrow afternoon? I've got something to show you that might make all the difference.'

'I'm snowed under with work. I must dash now. Try Tony Sweetman, he knows everyone.' He put the phone down, wondering if he'd made a terrible mistake. The idea of Bishop's Delight had taken root in his imagination, and plucking it out wasn't going to be easy.

He allowed twenty-four hours to pass before calling on Jane with a bunch of flowers specially made up by a florist whose services he'd had occasion to use more than once before.

'You're a right hypocrite, Woody. You think you can get around me with roses and gypsophila. I'm not stupid; I can see through you like a pane of glass.'

'It's my birthday on Saturday. I hope you wouldn't want me to spend it miserably on my own!'

'Surely you haven't fallen out with Mrs Maguire as well!'

'Look, Jane, I'm sorry. It will never happen again.'

At last he'd stumbled on the words that did the trick. It was always a matter of trial and error because the magic words varied from one crisis to the next. It was like having a fistful of keys and a door lock that never opened to the same key twice. She gave him a glass of wine and then another. They didn't watch television; they spent an hour planning a September holiday, debating whether they should go to Greece or Italy. At last he felt confident enough to kiss her, and her response inspired him to go even further. The chimes of midnight lent magic to their lovemaking. He wanted the chimes to go on and on, but understandably they came to an end. It was strange how imperfect life could be, even on the brink of perfection. The chimes had done their work, however. In the vastness of the emptiness they'd left behind he found himself falling headlong, as if through space. It occurred to him that he had, in fact, fallen in love.

'It's too late to go home,' he said. 'If you wouldn't mind, I'd like to stay the night.'

'I'll put on the alarm for five. You'll have to leave before anyone else is stirring.'

They were both as hungry for each other as if they had not eaten.

'We'll have to get married properly,' she said. 'We're more married already than many a married couple.'

He did not wait to think. 'We'll get married in September and make our holiday our honeymoon.'

'I'll be a good wife to you, Woody,' she said. 'I come from a long line of sensible women.'

'And I'll do my best to make you happy.' He lifted her off her feet and swung her around in the middle of the floor.

'My mother used to say, "You can't change people." I'd like to prove her wrong.'

'So you think I need changing?'

'Only by one or two degrees. It shouldn't be too difficult. An occasional touch on the tiller should do the trick. Do you think I need changing?' She raised her oval face and smiled.

'I fell in love with you because of how you are. Why should I want to upset such a delicate balance?'

'I won't try to change you either. We'll be ourselves; we'll rub along together as best we can.'

As arranged, he met Sweetman in Neary's on Friday. He arrived early so as to bag the corner table and sit with his back to the window while Sweetman faced the light. Sweetman turned up in newly pressed slacks and pink shirt, the very picture of dapper relaxation. He plonked his bulging shoulder bag down on the nearest chair and said that he was going to Tramore for the races and a dirty weekend.

'The turf, the surf, and Louise all together ... the very thought of it exhausts my fagged-out imagination.'

'Louise is good for a quickie if you're desperate. She never asks embarrassing questions and never fails to satisfy. Not my idea of a racing companion, though. Not even in Tramore.'

'But her name is revered among the racing fraternity. Her fame, you might say, has gone further than her hoof.'

'You mean Bishop's Delight, of course.' Sweetman's face lit up.

'More people have heard of it than have enjoyed it, I'd say.'

'Like the crock of gold at the bottom of the rainbow?'

'Or bird's-nest soup.'

'In my view it belongs in the realm of higher physics, $E=mc2$ and all that. I've even heard on the grapevine that she is thinking of patenting her little invention. But surely that can't be true! How can you keep other women from discovering it for themselves?'

'As I see it, there's no need for a patent. Bishop's Delight is a gift from heaven, peculiar to Louise alone.' He thought he might tempt Sweetman into revealing a little more of his thoughts.

'Like a wart where you wouldn't expect to find one?'

Sweetman declined to take the bait.

'More like a peculiarity of the anatomy, which happily becomes a seat of unparalleled pleasure.'

'Strange how it's never occurred to me to look at it like that before.'

'Take stock next time, and you'll see what I mean.'

'Pity it's such an exhausting business.' Sweetman was still giving nothing away.

'Especially for the man.'

139

'And for Louise herself, of course.'

'Isn't that why she only does it as a very special favour? Like the best things in life, it's strictly for the elect. It's the rarity of the thing that makes it so precious.'

Sweetman did something he'd never done before in his presence. He took a notebook from his shoulder bag and jotted down three words that Woody could not decipher from where he was sitting.

'Sorry about that,' he smiled. 'You reminded me of something. Something I must not forget. Too many irons in the fire. Do you ever feel you're spreading yourself too thin?'

'I like to keep it simple. A good girl for my spiritual needs, and a naughty girl to satisfy the beast in me. One of each is enough for any man. Dualism at its best, the secret of male contentment. The Victorians knew all about it.'

'I'm sorry, I must fly now,' Sweetman said. 'On a dirty weekend, nothing but nothing must go wrong. Next time I'll give you a blow-by-blowjob account, and the drinks will be on me.'

Woody's sense of disappointment threatened to overwhelm his sense of amusement. He had been looking forward to meeting him in order to discover something definite about Bishop's Delight, while instead Sweetman had come in the hope of prising an enlightening hint or two out of him. On parting, neither was any nearer the truth. Bishop's Delight was one of those things that vexed the carnal imagination, and in all probability would continue to vex it. It was such a pity that Jane was so possessive and so lacking in a man's sense of fun. All he would ask for was just one bite at the cherry, enough to keep the overleaping imagination from going berserk. He had always found that nothing damped down the fires of sexual fantasy more effectively than a healthy plunge into the cold grey waters of reality. But if he explained that to Jane, she might construe it as an implicit criticism of her charms. If only he could find happiness in solitude.... It was always other people and their inhibitions and inexplicable 'must-nots' that muddied the clear, bright stream of his free-roving thoughts.

19

His fifty-first birthday began as a perfect day. How was he to know that it would end in disaster? In the morning, Jane took him shopping in Grafton Street and bought him a pink shirt and green tie. When he balked at the thought of wearing pink and green, she told him firmly that pink was the fashion for men, that she'd read it in one of the colour supplements, and that anyway he was badly in need of a shirt that wasn't frayed at the cuffs and collar, and that from now on he must try to look young and 'with it'. There was nothing he could do but agree, though he knew he mustn't let Sweetman see him in a pink shirt because Sweetman was vain enough to imagine that he was copying his style.

They went to a film in the afternoon. Fortunately, it was one of those modern films with a lot of bonking, which gave him an excuse to kiss her every so often and feel the heat of her inner thigh against his hand. He had rarely felt happier. He had a tremendous erection throughout, but when he took her hand and placed it where he felt it should be, she whispered, 'Waste not, want not' in his ear. On the way home they stopped for a drink at a pub without music because they both felt in harmony with a greater music than any that ever came from a CD or jukebox.

'It's nearly dinner time,' he said. 'What do you say to a bite at the Trattoria Dante?'

'We've been gadding about all day. I'm fagged out. Maybe we should go home and rest for a bit.'

'If that's what you feel like doing.'

'I'd like to cook you something on your birthday, if I can find something cookable in your fridge.'

It was as if she'd read his thoughts. Eating wasn't on his mind. He just wanted to go to bed with her there and then, and as soon as they got home he said he'd have a shower to make himself sweet.

'You can join me if you like,' he added. 'Then we could soap each other up and down.'

'No, you go first. I think we'll save the soaping for our honeymoon.'

While he was in the shower, she had a look in the fridge, hoping to find something light because they'd had a good lunch in a little place in Temple Bar. While his fridge wasn't bare, it was no cornucopia. He was obviously in need of a sensible woman who knew better than to buy packaged crap from the supermarket. She still had not settled on anything in particular when the doorbell rang.

'I'm Louise, I'm a friend of Kevin's,' a smiling young woman said. 'He isn't expecting me. I happened to be passing and I thought I'd ring the bell.'

'Come in,' Jane said. 'He's freshening up at the moment. He shouldn't be too long.'

She didn't take her coat, but she pointed to the sofa, while she herself sat in the armchair opposite. Louise was quite good looking. She had a good figure and good legs, but there was something about the way she carried herself that shouted, 'Look at me!' Her black hair was nice and wavy, and she wasn't wearing too much make-up, perhaps because she felt there was no need.

'I expect you're an old friend of Kevin's.'

'Oh, yes. He got me my first job as a typist.'

'What do you do now?'

'I'm between jobs. I was a lingerie model for twelve years and now I'm training to be an actress.' She said all that as if it were far too much to say all together. Then she gave a little shake of the head so that her hair swayed sideways and back again. It was very agreeable to watch; Jane felt that if she were a man, she might be impressed.

'What is it like being a lingerie model?'

'It's difficult at first, but like everything else you get used to it.'

'All those men leering at you in your undies! Looking you up and down. It must be frightening.'

'No, it isn't like that at all. It's mostly women who come, and they don't leer, they just criticise.'

'But what do you think of while you're doing it?'

'You feel you're up here and they're down there. It gives you a great sense of power.'

'So why do you want to be an actress?'

'I think it's because you get sick of being yourself. I'd like to escape from my skin now and again. I like the idea of being someone else and having people think you're really that person and not your boring old self. It must give a great sense of release. Do you ever feel like that?'

'Well, not really. I'm fairly happy with my lot. I admire theatre actors, though. When I was at school, we were taken to see Anna Manahan acting the part of an old woman. I'll never forget how she rolled the "r" in the word "urine". Now I can never hear or say that word without thinking of Anna Manahan.'

'So you see why I want to be an actress. You live in the mind of everyone who's ever seen you. You're no longer leading one life but thousands, all at the same time.'

'Oh, hello, Louise.' Kevin came out of the bathroom towelling his hair.

'I'm sorry to barge in on you like this. I happened to be passing and I saw the light.'

'You've already met Jane, my fiancée. Have you found your ghost yet?' As he spoke, Jane looked at him as if he'd lost his marbles. 'Oh, Jane, I must explain. Louise is looking for a writer to ghost her memoirs.'

'I haven't come about that,' Louise said. 'I wanted to ask you about the photos. I found some more. I think you should see them.'

'The man to ask is Tony Sweetman. He knows everyone and the value of everything. I saw him only yesterday. He was wondering about the possibility of photos. Do you have his phone number?'

'Yes, I do. Sorry to have been a nuisance.' She got to her feet with an alacrity that showed dignity in hurt and grace at the same time. She smiled knowingly at Woody, and offered her hand to Jane.

'I enjoyed our conversation,' she said. 'When I become an actress, I'll remember to roll the "r" in "urine". We learn something new every day.'

Woody opened the door for her and said goodbye.

'She's got cheek. She's never been here before. She must have got my address from Sweetman.'

'What's all this about ghosts and photos?' Jane asked. 'It was Greek to me, or worse.'

He explained as best he could without giving too much away. He told her that he had known Louise since she was a schoolgirl and that she still saw him as a kind of uncle.

'She's far too pretty to be your niece. Have you got any more nieces you haven't told me about?'

'There's nothing between me and Louise, I can assure you.'

'Did you notice the way she keeps her legs while she's sitting—slanting like those models in the colour supplements?'

'She was a model for a while. I suppose some of it must have rubbed off.'

He felt uneasy. He could see that Jane was suspicious, and he did not know how to reassure her. It was a time for originality, but his imagination was jaded from years of cynicism.

'I wish she wouldn't keep pestering me,' he said. 'I keep telling her that Sweetman is the money-bags she's looking for, but she refuses to take a hint.'

'Ghosts, photos, money-bags. What is all this about?'

'Louise is looking for a journalist to ghost her memoirs. She's hoping to get her book serialised in the Sunday papers, and she thinks the photos in her possession would be a help.'

'And where do you come in?'

'She asked me to recommend a suitable journalist, and I suggested Sweetman. That's the sum total of my involvement.'

'But why does she think anyone would be interested in her memoirs?'

'Apparently, she knows a lot of bigwigs in the fashion world. She says she wants to tell everyone about what goes on behind the scenes.'

'Do you mean between the sheets?'

'I don't really know. I didn't enquire and she didn't tell me.'

'You're an innocent, Woody, or you must think I am. Don't you see what's going on? She plans to publish her photos of sex orgies, and you're an accessory before the fact.'

She collapsed on the sofa and burst into tears. He sat down beside her and put his arm round her shoulders.

'You mustn't imagine things, Jane. Louise just comes to me for good advice.'

'She's a hooker, if ever there was one. Ghostwriters, photos, money-bags ... it's all about sex and blackmail. Kevin, how could you do such a thing to me? And what do you want with an ordinary down-to-earth girl like me?'

'Jane, I love you. I want to spend my life with you.'

'Now I know why you bought me red underwear for Christmas. You said it was because Santa Claus wears red, and you made me parade round the bedroom in red knickers. It was because you'd seen her in them. You make me feel grubby. How could you do such a thing to a simple, clean-living girl?'

'The things you're imagining wouldn't occur to me in a month of Sundays.' He took her hand and kissed it.

'Don't touch me. I don't want to catch some terrible disease.' She got up and went for her coat.

'Jane!' he said feebly, knowing that it was no good.

As the door closed behind her, he sank into the sofa and down into his boots. The unexpected turn of events had defeated him, and he hadn't the imagination to find words that might put things right. 'Bugger Louise,' he said. 'She's wrecked me and fucked me this time, and I won't forget it.'

He'd never felt so unhappy. She wouldn't take his telephone calls, and in the evenings, when he waited outside her flat after work, she wouldn't stop to talk to him. He spent hours writing letters, searching in vain for the magic words of contrition. He sent her text messages, but she refused to answer them. Finally, he sent her a text in capitals:

I'M SUICIDAL. HAVE MERCY ON ME.

It was the last throw of the dice. He waited and waited with his mobile on the desk before him. He had given up hope when finally her reply arrived: Meet Tratt Dante tomorrow 7.

Now that he'd cracked it, it all seemed so simple. Why hadn't he thought of it before? He still felt vulnerable, though; he could hardly believe how much his happiness depended on her. It was an undesirable state of affairs since she could withdraw her love on a whim or for no intelligible reason. His life had always run so smoothly because for years he'd taken care never to become emotionally involved with another human being. It made sense for a busy man not to be subject to every change of mood and female vagary, yet now he had to admit that his happiness depended entirely on Jane. He wondered what Sweetman would make of his predicament. He wouldn't tell him, of course. Come to think of it, he couldn't and wouldn't tell any man. Yet surely it must be a problem common to all men. He couldn't imagine Sweetman falling in love. He kept his life simple, probably because he couldn't bear the psychological strain.

He booked one of the two alcove tables in the Trattoria Dante to ensure privacy and a respectable distance from the banalities of other conversations. Jane was sensitive to her surroundings, and this was one of those occasions when nothing must go wrong. He arrived at six-fifty, and immediately sent her a text to that effect in case she might think it a requirement of etiquette to arrive late. He had devoted a lot of thought to this encounter. He had noted every conceivable conversational permutation and thought out a suitable response to each. He would normally have ordered a drink to be going on with while he waited, but on this occasion he thought it best to give her no excuse to accuse him of insensitivity, boorishness or worse.

He waved to her as she entered, and she smiled, which was a good sign. She had taken care over her dress and hair— another good sign. She had done it all for his benefit, and he felt pleased. She was good looking in a quiet way, and she dressed quietly. No one would ever say that she was loud. She sat facing him, though he'd have preferred her to sit next to him.

'What have you been doing?'

'Reading your letters and texts. I had time for little else.'

'It hasn't been easy, Jane.'

'We won't talk about that now. We'll look at the menu to find out what's on offer.'

He ordered drinks, a spritzer for her and a gin and tonic for himself. She said she wasn't hungry and that one course was all she needed. She ordered *spaghetti alla puttanesca* because it seemed 'appropriate to the occasion,' as she put it, and he ordered *spaghetti alle vongole*, though he fancied the *puttanesca* but didn't want her to think he was grovelling. When he ordered a bottle of Bardolino, she told him that one glass of the house wine would be enough for her. It was untypical of her to be so abstemious. He had been hoping that one glass would lead to another, and a slackening of any residual tension.

'Now,' she said, when the waiter had gone, 'we must get down to the business of the evening. You have one view and I have another. You feel I've misjudged you, and I feel you've let me down. We both feel we're right, and we won't resolve our differences by force of argument.'

'I agree entirely,' he said. 'There's no point in accusation. All I'd like is a second chance to prove that I'm serious.'

'Serious about what?'

'I love you, Jane. I've had nothing but misery since you left me. My life isn't worth living. I just can't go on like this.'

'Neither can I.'

'The answer is obvious then,' he said. 'We must find a lasting way to express our love for each other.'

'Precisely. This is a spiritual problem. We're just not on the same wavelength. You're not receiving me and I'm not receiving you.'

The conversation had taken a turn he had not anticipated. He thought it best to wait till she had shown her hand.

'So what do you suggest?' he asked.

'Three days in Lough Derg. That will give us both time to think.'

'You mean a boating holiday?'

'No, the other Lough Derg, the one in Donegal.'

'Saint Patrick's Purgatory?'

'Yes. It's a three-day stint, fasting, praying, and walking barefoot around the penitential beds. It isn't difficult, provided you're serious about your intentions.'

'But what's the purpose of it?'

'Self-discovery and self-renewal. The person who comes out is never the same as the person who went in.'

'Sounds interesting,' he murmured, because he could not think of anything better to say.

'Will you do it with me?'

'I'll do it,' he promised, while wondering what on earth she could be up to.

'I'll make the arrangements. We'll go in at lunchtime on a Friday and come out at lunchtime the following Monday. With any luck I'll see you in a different light, and you'll see me as I really am.'

'Sounds a bit scary. I don't want anything to change. I want to keep seeing you as I see you now, the beautiful young woman I love, and want to keep loving you for the rest of my life.'

'Trust me, Woody. I also want to spend my life with you, but first I must love you wholeheartedly, without a shadow of doubt in my mind.'

'I feel like one of those ancient heroes who were given tests at puberty to prove their manhood.'

'You still don't understand. You won't be doing it for me. You'll be doing it to cleanse yourself of all pretence and falsehood and discover the true Woody.'

'And are you doing it to discover the true Jane?'

'I'm doing it to discover both the true Jane and the true Woody.'

What could he say? He had played his best card and she'd trumped it. There was no point in fruitless argument. It was the story of Cuchulainn's entry into manhood all over again, but he would not be deterred. She herself had taken the test before. If she could do it, so could he.

She didn't mention Lough Derg again. They talked about the sultry weather and a score of other innocuous topics. She said she didn't want coffee and that she was looking forward to an early night. As he walked her to her bus stop, he became aware of an other-worldly wall between them. He could see her, hear her, even touch her, but he could not get through to her. He felt relieved when she waved him goodbye from the bus.

He walked home because he needed time to think. What fit of fanaticism had come over her? She had always struck him as a reasonable and level-headed girl. Though well capable of defending her corner, she was remarkably even-tempered. She didn't suffer from mood swings, she didn't throw tantrums, she never resorted to emotional blackmail, and he had never known her to sulk. Her only fault was invincible intransigence. He had seen her as the perfect woman for a journalist on a modest salary. Surely this business of Lough Derg was a temporary aberration. As he put his house key in the Yale lock, he said aloud, 'If only I can get her back into bed again, I'll make short work of all this nonsense.'

20

They set out on an overcast morning in early August and drove north. Sitting next to him, she seemed happy and at ease. There was no sense of tension between them; they could have been going on holiday to enjoy a few days of quiet relaxation in the country.

'Are you looking forward to Lough Derg?' she asked.

'It's a little adventure. I don't know what's in store for me, and I can't wait to find out.'

'It's the kind of place that could change your life. That's the whole point of the journey. If you go in with a closed mind, you'll come out with a closed mind. But if you go in with a mind that is wide open, you'll probably come out renewed. The secret is to be receptive, to empty the tired old self and make room for whatever falls down from above to fill the vacuum. I hope it rains on us while we're on the island because I think rain is symbolic, since it falls from the sky.'

'You should have warned me. I'd have brought my anorak.'

'You heathen! I can see I have a job on my hands.'

She smiled as she said it, which was a good sign. She was obviously pleased that he had agreed to come, and he felt pleased that she was happy. They listened to the radio for a while in silence. Finally, she said that modern songs were humourless and flat.

'Do you know any old songs?' she asked.

'I'm not a singer, but I can say the words.'

'If you begin, I'll do my best to join in,' she promised.

'*As I went out one morning, it being in the month of May,*' he said.

'*A farmer and his daughter I spied upon the way,*' she sang.

'*And the daughter sat down calmly to the milking of her cow,*'

'*Saying, "I will and I must get married, for the humour is on me now,"*' she sang.

She slapped his knee and laughed. 'You're the very devil, getting me to sing a thing like that. But I don't mind. It shows we still love each other, and that we haven't lost our sense of humour.'

'We'll stop there,' he smiled. 'It might be tempting Providence to sing the last verse.'

'What is the last verse?' she asked.

'*I'm sorry I ever got married, for the humour is off me now.*'

'I'm not superstitious.' She laid her head against his shoulder. 'If you tell me the words, I'll sing it for you.'

As they drove through Pettigo, the sky darkened. With thirteen other pilgrims, they waited on the pier for the open boat to return from the island. They found seats near the stern. He sat next to her with his thigh pressing against hers, and held her hand. As they pushed off, the heavens opened with a clap of thunder. It wasn't just a shower. It rained all the way across. 'Rainy Donegal, we should have gone to Lourdes instead,' someone said. 'I don't mind. It will wash us clean,' Jane whispered in his ear. He said nothing. This by all appearances was going to be one of those weekends.

Before leaving Dublin he had told himself that he must on no account give her cause for complaint. He wasn't a religious man. He believed that life was governed by chance and little else, that it was entirely meaningless, and that the best he could do was to pursue his own personal happiness without interfering unduly with anyone else's. His happiness depended on regaining Jane's love, and he was willing to do anything short of murder to achieve it. If she saw this caper as a test of his love, he would make sure that he passed with flying colours. All things considered, he was getting off lightly. A weekend on a penitential island was a piece of cake compared with half a lifetime in the gulag or Robben Island.

'We won't cling to each other,' she said as they landed. 'We'll go our separate ways and compare notes when we meet again. That way we'll have two experiences instead of one.'

'You needn't worry. If I see you in the distance, I won't blow you a kiss. I'll just wink at you instead.'

In spite of his feelings of goodwill, walking about barefoot on wet stones made him question whether Jane was all there. The soles of his feet were tender, but so presumably were hers. The repetitive prayers were another problem. Going around and around the crosses and penitential beds saying the same prayers over and over again lulled him into a kind of stupor. Furthermore, he didn't know all the prayers that the other pilgrims took for granted. He knew the Our Father and the Hail Mary, but for the life of him he couldn't remember the Apostles' Creed. Still, he had to make an effort. He had to be seen to be doing what everyone else was doing. He mustn't draw attention to himself by behaving with anything that did not look like piety and reverence.

Curiously, the night vigil didn't worry him unduly. He fell into a kind of trance, which was more like a dream peopled by Tony Sweetman, Jim Maguire and Bill MacBride, Jane, Anna and Louise. The basilica was warm and dimly lit. Pilgrims walked around and around it as the earth goes round the sun. There was a strong wind, which blew from all directions. No matter where he went, he seemed to be facing into it. No wonder the place was called St Patrick's Purgatory. If you wanted time to think, this was the place to come to because there was nothing else to do. You had to think to keep your sanity. It was four o'clock in the morning. He saw a lone figure on a bench having a quiet fag, and he made for what he thought might be a fellow sufferer.

'I suppose I shouldn't be smoking,' she said.

'I don't mind. We all come here for our own idea of a quiet drag.'

'I'm sure you're right.' The moon glimmered on her teeth as she smiled. 'What's your idea of a quiet drag?'

'Thinking about things I wouldn't normally have time to think about.'

'You're lucky. I come here to get away from my husband. He beats me, the brute.'

For a moment he was at a loss. 'Why should anyone want to beat you?' he asked finally.

'He beats me because he enjoys beating me. Some men are animals.'

'But surely you should go to the police.'

'The police are brutes as well, even bigger and thicker than my husband. I come here to pray for his conversion. It's the only hope.'

'Conversion from which religion?' he enquired.

'From Catholicism. I was brought up in the Church of Ireland. I became a Catholic when I married him. I was too young to know what I was letting myself in for.'

Suddenly, he found himself looking around. What if Jane should find him in conversation with another woman, especially a good-looking young woman who saw him as her father confessor?

'If I were you, I'd run away,' he said.

'He'd come after me. He loves me, you see. That's the problem. Excessive love is worse than no love at all.'

'You're wrong there,' he said. 'Some people come here to pray for love, and I'm one of them.' He got up and told her that he was going for a turn around the basilica.

'I hope you find the love you're looking for,' she said. 'And I hope you'll be happy when you do.'

Like Jane, he had come to the island fasting. He'd been given a meagre meal of dry toast and black tea some time after their arrival. He felt that he should be feeling hungry by now, but the toast must have expanded in his stomach to achieve a kind of multiplication that he had no intention of calling miraculous. He wouldn't tell that to Jane because she would see it as the kind of thinking more appropriate to an atheist than a true son of St Patrick. He would have to keep his scepticism under wraps and say as little as possible about the kind of mindless pap the priests were peddling in their sermons. He wasn't against sermons as such; he just longed to hear something intelligent and original, something that wasn't the equivalent of Sweetman's journalism. He refused to believe that all priests were stupid, yet most of them seemed to switch off their brain as soon as they mounted the pulpit. They talked about shepherds and sheep, and they probably saw the sheep as stupid. That, surely, was a mistake. In every fold was a sheep or two that could give instruction to the shepherd. The needs of the wide awake should not be sacrificed to the needs of the somnolent majority.

'The hungry sheep look up and are not fed,' he found himself saying aloud.

'Surely you're not weakening already?' Jane, who had come up behind him, took his hand in hers.

'I was only trying to make sense of myself,' he smiled.

'You were looking across at the far shore. I thought you might be planning an escape.'

156

'Nothing as dramatic as that. I was thinking about thee and me.'

'Your prayer has been answered. Here I am. Have you been to confession yet?'

'No,' he said, doing his best to conceal his alarm.

'Neither have I. We'll go together. It will be a special occasion for us both.'

She led him into the basilica, and they took their place in the queue. This was a test of his bona fides. She was bound to note any show of reluctance or impiety. The queue was quite long. They had a good half-hour to prepare for the ordeal. Going first, she took so long that he felt the confessor must be giving her a very hard time indeed. When his turn came, he'd had ample time to rehearse his innocuous story. The priest was an old man with a few wisps of white hair hanging down over his ears. His soutane had red buttons down the front, which caused Woody to wonder if he was about to be shriven by no less a personage than a monsignor. He listened to his story with his right hand cupping his ear, then gave him a word of kindly advice and finally his penance and absolution. 'Say a prayer for me,' he said. 'I probably need it more than you do.'

Woody felt deeply ashamed of himself. He felt so ashamed that he was worried in case Jane might suspect something.

'What penance did you get?' she asked when they were alone again.

'One Our Father and one Hail Mary.'

'You got off lightly. He gave me a whole rosary. Are you sure you told him everything?'

'Quite sure.'

'About what we'd been doing together?'

'Priests are harder on women than men. They see women as daughters of Eve, the first and greatest sinner.'

'Do you believe that?'

'Of course not. We're all in this mess together. We can only try to make the best of it.' He felt a right old hypocrite, but it was all in a good cause. He would make a caring husband and she would be a loving wife. Surely a little dishonesty was permissible to ensure the greater good.

'Are you hungry?' she asked.

'Yes, but it doesn't worry me.'

'You put me to shame, Woody. I keep asking myself if all this fasting can be good for me.'

'What worries me is the lack of sleep. I keep thinking about a lovely feather bed.'

'I must leave you, Woody. I can see I'm putting unholy thoughts in your head.'

He was delighted that she had come to talk to him. In her innocence she saw him as a fellow sinner, not as a predator whose dearest wish was to 'sin' with her again. The curious thing about Lough Derg was that her religious devotion only fuelled his desire. He didn't mind his hunger for a sumptuous meal. What he minded was his hunger to feel once again the urgency of her burning appetite for love.

In his reverie he came upon an old man sitting alone with eyes that watered as if he were holding back tears.

'Is this your first time here?' He sat down next to him.

'It's only my second. My wife, may she rest, came here on her own for over twenty years. I lost her two years ago. Now I come in her place. She speaks to me in these smooth stones. She walked on them barefoot, and so do I. As I go around the basilica I think I hear her whispering in the wind. I suppose you're a regular?'

'No, I came with my girlfriend. It's my first time.'

'Keep coming with her while you can because you won't always have her. Life is like that. We don't know when we're happy.'

He left the old man and went back into the basilica. He wanted to sit next to Jane, but she was nowhere to be seen. He needed her comforting hand in his and the reassurance of being next to her. These were things he had been taking for granted. The old man was right. We can only know the light of happiness by looking back on it from the dark valley of despair. He told himself that be must never take Jane's love for granted again.

'Are you pleased you came with me?' she asked, looking back on the island from the boat.

'It has made me think,' he said.

'What about?'

'You and me. What's important and what isn't.'

Satisfied, she rested her head against his shoulder. Lough Derg had taught him the magic words that could set her mind at rest and make her happy. They were worth discovering, those words. As in a Euclid exam, knowing the theorems was half the battle.

'We'll spend the night in Sligo,' he said as they drove off. He had been imagining a comfortable hotel and a double bed in an airy room overlooking the river.

'We'll ask for single rooms,' she said. 'Otherwise we'd be sinning before the fact.'

'You should have been a theologian, Jane. You make up new sins as you go along.'

'We'll compromise,' she smiled. 'We'll ask for a double room with twin beds.'

'We have only one double room left and it has a double bed,' the receptionist said. 'It's the arts festival week, you see.'

'We'll take it,' Jane said, as seriously as if she were about to undergo a rigorous endurance test.

They enjoyed what was left of the afternoon. They went for a walk along the river and had a drink in Hargadon's, once a genuine old pub that spoke of a life unknown to the Celtic Tiger generation, now renewed to meet the noisy demands of the uncultivated young. They were supposed to fast till midnight, but Jane in a moment of leniency gave them both dispensation from further self-denial.

'We won't gorge ourselves,' she said. 'We'll just have something light for our stomachs' sake.'

She said that she felt tired, that they should have an early night, and he felt inclined to agree. She had a shower and washed her hair, and he thought it best to do likewise. It was eleven when they finally got into bed. They stretched out side by side to read their newspapers. Although he had not seen a newspaper for three days, his mind was no longer on the news. He was doing his best to forget about his erection because he knew that it was not in his interest to rush things. However, he could not conceal from himself his sense of absurdity. Any onlooker would think they had been married for several centuries, and that their passion for each other had finally dimmed. He waited and waited. Finally, she said, 'My eyes are closing. We'll call it a day.'

In the darkness he held her and kissed her. He kissed her neck, lips, and closed eyes. He put his hand into her nightdress and touched her breasts. Her whole body stiffened. Even her breasts hardened, he could swear. She was sobbing in fits against his chest.

'Oh, Woody, it's no good,' she whimpered.

'What's wrong, Jane?'

'I don't know. I just can't do it any more.'

'Let me hold you. We'll be quiet for a while.'

'It's your touch, Woody. It gives me pins and needles in the wrong place.'

'It doesn't make any sense.'

'I'm sorry, Woody. It's all my fault. Maybe I'll be all right if you give me time.'

Finally, he fell asleep. She had already showered before he woke up. She said the sun was shining outside and that it promised to be a lovely day. At breakfast she put her hand on his and smiled.

'I was adrift last night,' she said. 'I was tired. I'd lost the thread. I didn't know who or where I was.'

'We were both tired. I slept like a log. If you hadn't woken me, I'd still be asleep.'

'I'll make it up to you, Woody, I promise.'

'You needn't worry, Jane. We were both on a high. It will take us a week or maybe longer to get back down to earth.'

'I knew you'd understand. You're very special to me, Woody. I wouldn't like anything to come between us.'

They sang more songs and ballads on the way home. She seemed cheerful enough, but somehow he could not help feeling diminished. As they parted, she asked for 'four days to get back to normal'. She said that she would come around to see him on Saturday, but when Saturday came it was the same story. As he saw it, her mind was willing but her body had rebelled against him. He couldn't understand why, and he was reluctant to ask her. She cooked him meals and bought him a new shirt and tie, but still she could not make love.

'I think it's because of Louise,' she said finally. 'Whenever you touch me, I think of her and how she must have felt under the weight of all those men.'

'I don't understand,' he said. 'Louise means nothing to me. She asked me to help her and I declined. I've never been to bed with her and I have no wish to go to bed with her.'

'This is not about cheating. It's about misplaced love. All I ever wanted was an ordinary, everyday man, and I thought I'd found one.'

After that they drifted apart without either anger or recrimination. There was no formal goodbye. Her love had died. There was nothing more to say.

For a long time afterwards he felt that he had lost his anchorage. In time he would recover it, of course, but for the moment he was only going through the motions of living. Jane belonged to an older Ireland, an Ireland of Masses and novenas, the Ireland of his father and grandfather, which he'd fondly imagined had vanished forever. She was a revenant from a legendary past, and perhaps that was why she had made such an impression on his yearning imagination. In her unassumingly intuitive way she created for him an illusion of familial continuity, bridging the gulf between the old and the new.

21

He spent the best part of the afternoon in Maguire's study while Anna worked upstairs. She came down at around four and invited him to stay to dinner. When he said he'd love to, she told him not to get too excited, that it was only cold salmagundi. Apparently, she'd roasted a chicken and a joint of beef earlier in the week and still had some of both left over. She had eggs, anchovies and salad in the fridge, and she was wondering if he'd mind nipping out to the greengrocer's for a couple of onions. He couldn't help being amused by her knack of putting questions to him that invited only one answer.

He didn't mind. He had nothing more urgent to do. Talking to someone would keep him from thinking about Jane, and, as it happened, he enjoyed the salmagundi, Maguire's wine, and her somewhat fey conversation. When he told her that he'd been to Lough Derg, she asked him if it was for a dirty weekend. He wondered if she'd been drinking all afternoon; it was not the kind of thing she'd say without the help of a whisky or two. Still, he couldn't help smiling. In her eccentric way she had hit on a truth that had not revealed itself to him before.

'Why do you associate Lough Derg with dirty weekends?' he asked.

'It used to be a great place for couples going through a bad patch. They'd spend three days fasting and praying, hoping they'd come out at the end with a keener appetite for each other. Afterwards they couldn't wait to get to Enniskillen and grab a packet of condoms for the night. Now that we're sexually emancipated in the Republic, there's no need to go to Enniskillen any more. You can buy your condoms in any chemist and spend the night in Bundoran by the sea. Was that what you did?'

'No, we got as far as Sligo before succumbing to temptation.'

'But what took you to Lough Derg in the first place? I hadn't put you down as a Holy Joe.'

'I went to please Jane.'

'And did it work for you?'

'It worked for her but not for me. She found out she wasn't in love with me.'

'Were you in love with her?'

'I'm very fond of her.'

'I'm sorry, Kevin. I suppose you miss her.'

'She was a large part of my life, though I didn't know it at the time.'

'It's always the way. We never know happiness; we can only recall it.'

'I've known happiness. Jane and I had some good times together, and I knew then that they were good times and wouldn't last forever.'

'Love means a calm sea for some, and storm and shipwreck for others. Dull people know what they want, and what they get is all they ever want. Restless souls are never satisfied. They yearn and agonise and imagine the scores of lives they might be leading but cannot.'

'I don't think I agree,' he said. 'I wouldn't call myself restless, or even imaginative. I'm just unlucky, but I won't let it get to me. What happened to me chimes in perfectly with my idea of life, which is entirely meaningless and for the most part frivolous.'

'You're very wrong. We humans need meaning. Where there is no meaning, we make it up. If I wrote a meaningless fairy tale, no child would want to read it. By insisting on meaninglessness, Kevin, you're denying yourself happiness. That's my view. Now kiss me to show there's no ill feeling between us.'

She pointed to her cheek with her forefinger. He kissed her on the lips instead.

'Now don't get fresh with me, Woody,' she smiled. 'You should know by now when I'm joking.'

She went to the sideboard and came back with a bottle of Talisker. Her supply of malt Scotch seemed endless; she had a fresh bottle for every occasion.

'Here's to Jim, wherever he is!' She raised her glass. 'I'll say this much for him. He had good taste in whisky.'

They spent the evening talking about Jim, but she didn't say anything he hadn't heard her say before. Finally, she reached across the table and took his hand.

'I'll ask you two questions, Kevin, and I'll expect a truthful answer to both of them. The first is what do you really think happened to Jim?'

It was a question she'd asked him before, and he paused for a moment before answering.

'He went out fishing and the sea turned choppy. He ran out of petrol and couldn't make it back to the pier. The wind was blowing him farther from land, so he decided to swim ashore. Unfortunately, he didn't make it.'

'What about the oars? Surely he could have rowed back.'

'The loss of the oars is a mystery. I just don't know the answer.'

'Then, why all this speculation, if it's as cut and dried as you say?'

'It's journalism, Anna. Where there is no cause, we must invent one.'

'But surely all journalism isn't fiction?'

'There's an element of fiction in all of it. It's the search for meaning you were on about earlier. Readers demand meaning, and journalists invent it because it's in such short supply.'

'Now for my other question. Were you ever in love with me, Kevin, or did I just imagine it?'

'You were my first love, Anna. I don't mind telling you that now. It took me a while to get over it, but I did. It all happened a long time ago. I don't even remember what it felt like, but I do remember your auburn hair with a brown clip on one side and the orange blouse you used to wear to the office.'

'Thank you for telling me. I often think about those times, but I could never be sure. Now I'd like you to spend the night with me. We won't make love, but we might find comfort in each other's warmth.'

She told him that she would go up first, and to give her half an hour to prepare for bed. When she had gone, he poured himself another Scotch. He felt that he had lost control of his life. Jane had set him adrift like a cockle shell on a tide that would carry him back and forth and deposit him blindly on some nameless shore. He had lost Jane and all volition to make good the loss; he had even lost the impulse to complete what he had once seen as his magnum opus. Now he must wait high and dry until a spring tide might happily set him afloat again.

He found her sitting up in bed reading. She peered at him over her glasses and said she'd switch off the light if he wished to undress in the dark. He told her that he always undressed with the light on, and that even if she looked she'd probably see nothing she had not seen before. Smiling, she said she was no peeping Tom. Then she began wondering why peeping was a male preserve and why there were no peeping Millies or Mollies. He got in beside her and put his arm around her, and they lay together for what seemed an eternity in the dark.

'It's a great comfort for me to lie with a man again,' she said. 'Jim and I stopped being intimate on my forty-first birthday. He said that morning he'd take me out to dinner. He was late home. I waited twenty minutes, and when he kissed me in the hallway I said half-jokingly that he smelt of a weird kind of perfume. I felt him stiffen in his pinstripe suit. I had committed an unforgivable sin; I'd let him see he'd been found out. He never troubled me for sex again.'

'Was it difficult for you?'

'It was a chilling rejection and I shall never forget it. If we'd had a row, I might have understood. Instead we had pointed silence. I call it "pointed" rather than "pregnant" because it was so sharply piercing.'

'You've been very loyal to him, in spite of everything.'

'I made allowances, thinking that one day he'd come back to me and I'd have him to myself again.'

He kissed her on the lips and neck and put his hand on her breast.

'Tonight we'll be quiet,' she said. 'I've told you about Jim. I'd like to hear about Jane.'

There was a weeping in his chest that made him hesitate. He did not trust himself to speak for fear of betraying his feelings.

'Jane worked in a solicitor's office,' he said finally. 'She had no legal training, but she had picked up a lawyer's way of looking at things. She expected a sentence to have one meaning and only one. She was particular and precise, whereas I am content to live with ambiguity. That was the difference that came between us and finally wrecked us.'

'But how did it wreck you, as you choose to put it? There must have been some incident that tipped the balance.'

'She wanted certainty. She didn't want ever to experience doubt. She was very possessive and very suspicious. If I as much as spoke to another woman, she suspected a liaison.'

'Do you think you're better rid of her?'

'No, I don't. Without her my life is … flat.'

'You're still in love, Woody. I think you should go to her and beg forgiveness on bended knee.'

'But I've done nothing wrong. Besides, it would do no good.'

'When you put your hand on my breast just now, did you wish it were hers?'

'No, I just wished I'd got my hand on yours thirty years ago. If I had, my life would have been different.'

'I can see why you're a freelance journalist. You wouldn't be happy in a bank, or indeed in any job where you had to please someone. You just want to please yourself.'

'It's what we're all doing in our own peculiar ways.'

'I've enjoyed our little talk. Now we both know each other. We know what we can expect and what we can't. I hope you'll stay the night. I want to wake up at three and put over my hand to find you there.'

He stayed the night, sleeping heavily after the whisky. In the morning, as he shaved with Maguire's razor, he felt like the victim of a weird dream. Anna was not an easy woman to handle. She had a way of attracting whoever came within the glow of her candle. He would have to make sure his wings didn't get singed. What he needed now was the unconsidered comfort of a woman who would ask no awkward questions while making the kind of conversation that required neither effort nor ingenuity. Anna's questions last night had severely tested his powers of impromptu invention. It was not the kind of test he wished to undergo every night of the week. He didn't have to think twice. In the afternoon he phoned Louise and invited her out for a drink.

One drink led to another. She seemed to be enjoying herself; he felt that he had been given a rare glimpse of what it was like to be Louise. She didn't like Sweetman. She felt he was an iron man with neither flaw nor feeling.

'Surely he must suffer from metal fatigue now and again,' he joked.

'I'd like to smelt him down and make him into something I could stamp on with my stilettos.'

'But I thought he was ghosting your book?'

'He's milking my mind rather than writing down the things I want to say. He doesn't see me as an ordinary human being but as some sort of freak. He keeps asking me questions I don't want to answer.'

'What sort of questions?'

'Intimate questions about the things that made me what I am. I just want to write a book about the interesting people I've met, not what they did but what they said. I don't want to write down every stray thought that comes into my mind. I have no control over my thoughts. They're a nightmare; most of the time I want to forget them. I certainly don't want to preserve them for posterity. I'd be much happier if you were doing the writing because I feel I could trust you.'

'Sweetman is a first-class journalist. He's far more successful than me.'

'He's out for himself. I think he must be writing two books, one for himself and one for me. He keeps probing me about Maguire, what he was like and if he was interested in kinky sex. Now that isn't the kind of book I want to write. I don't see myself as a tart, but Sweetman does.'

'Sweetman and I have a curious relationship. I'm sure he's as suspicious of me as I am of him, but we meet once a week because it suits us. He finds out things from me and I find out things from him, and neither of us knows what the other has found out. He has a finger in every pie that's cooking. He's interested in Maguire, and who wouldn't be? He was a complex personality and a most unusual politician.'

'I'd agree with you there. He used to come to me all tied up. He said I had the knack of letting him "slip his mooring".

He didn't come just for sex. Sometimes he came to talk. I'd make him a cup of camomile tea, and he'd sit on the sofa for an hour with his hand on my knee. He was like a roguish uncle to me. He once told me my back reminded him of his favourite odalisque. When I said I had no idea what he was talking about, he promised to take me to an art gallery in Paris one day and point her out to me. He thought that funny. He laughed, and I laughed too.'

'Maguire would have done well in an artistic walk of life, had he chosen one. Sadly, he entered politics. For him, it was a wrong turning. Politics is for people who are capable of nothing else.'

'That isn't Sweetman's view. He says politics is more of an art than a craft, and that politicians live a life of the imagination so intense that artists can't even begin to imagine it.'

'How can you remember all that detail, Louise?'

'I have the gift of total recall. What I lack is the knack of winnowing it for sense. If I wrote a book, it would look like two-ton Tessie. You journalists know how to slim Tessie down and give her a sexy figure.'

'You must never underrate yourself. There will always be those who will do it for you.'

'Like Maguire, you have a generous mind, Woody. Why don't you come back with me? We'll pick up a king-size pizza and share it. Then you can sit beside me on the sofa with your hand on my knee and talk to me about all sorts of crazy things. I'd like that for a change.'

He began as she suggested, and ended up in bed with her. For the space of an hour she made him feel he was the only man in her world. She was alert and attentive in a jokey way, as if they were both engaged in a childish prank. While she was in the bathroom, he put €100 in an envelope and left it on her night table.

'You shouldn't have done that, Woody,' she said, 'but sadly I need it.'

'I was down in the mouth and you made me happy. That's a pearl beyond any price.'

'You and I are two of a kind. We understand each other because we're both outsiders.' She took his hand and kissed him. It was one of her lingering kisses that stayed with him all the way home.

He could understand what Maguire had seen in her. It wasn't just her face and finely moulded figure, but her darting intelligence that sparkled as it darted and never lit for long in any one place. As he crossed the Liffey, a surge of happiness washed through him. He felt human again after more than six months of misery in a grey, cold underworld that had not been of his making.

22

Woody came to see her twice a week now, on Tuesdays and Thursdays. She usually gave him dinner on Thursdays, and more often than not he stayed the night. They were not lovers, but she could see that he was fond of her. She had come to look forward to Thursdays, and she always made an effort to cook something special. His tastes were simple; he made no demands she could not meet, and he was happy sharing a bottle of wine and enjoying one or two fingers of Scotch before bedtime. Still, she did not wish to give the impression that her culinary repertoire was unimaginative. Last week she had cooked chilli con carne, which he loved. This week she would give him *polpettini* in a cheese and tomato sauce. As it was Wednesday, she went to the butcher's to buy minced lamb and pick up the other ingredients at the supermarket. She felt quite exhausted by the time she got back. She poured herself a revivifying Scotch and flopped down in the nearest armchair.

The sex diaries were on her mind. They had awakened in her a belated curiosity about the world 'out there'—about her own unlived life and about the hidden life hinted at in Jim's enigmatic jottings. Like most women of her generation, she had missed out on life's great adventure. At twenty-one she was a simple country girl who saw her future in a choice between two men she knew next to nothing about. Eager to turn to the next page, she failed to see life as a once-only opportunity that must on no account be squandered. Jim didn't squander his opportunities. He travelled widely and learned while she stayed at home writing stories for other people's children. She had been robbed of a life that should have been as rich and as varied as Jim's. In many ways she was still as innocent as the twenty-one-year-old girl he took to Paris on honeymoon thirty years ago. Was she now too old to learn what real life was like? Was it too late to make up for thirty years of not knowing and a life as blind as a pupa's in a cocoon? And was Woody the kind of man she could turn to with confidence?

In many ways he was a mystery. Though he could talk the hind leg off a donkey, he gave very little of himself away. He would talk endlessly about people he'd met and what they had said without ever divulging what he thought of them. At times she wondered if he was all memory without any firm views of his own, yet as soon as he sat down in front of a keyboard he became as opinionated as any politician. He was lively company, amusing and even witty by turns. He knew when to listen and how to disagree without giving offence. He had a kind of charm she did not associate with hard-nosed journalists. He was a vast improvement on the abominable Sweetman. In some respects he was an improvement on Jim.

Unlike Jim, he did not drop off as soon as his head hit the pillow. They would lie side by side and talk in the dark about old times until one of them no longer responded. They were like a long-married couple, taking each other's affection for granted, feeling that there was no longer need for anything fevered or frenzied in the night. They had fallen into a routine of her making, from which there seemed to be no escape. His implacable courtesy was a sign of his affection for her. At times she yearned for change, but could not imagine how it might be brought about.

It occurred to her that his relationship with Jane, whom he still mentioned on occasion, had run along similar lines. Quite possibly he was one of those men who needed to be lured into action. A forward woman would take him in hand without feeling that she was going beyond the bounds of propriety and her own nature. He had told her about Jane. It would be interesting to have a similar account of him from Jane's point of view. She was younger than Woody. She probably saw him as old-fashioned and hopelessly dilatory, the kind of man her mother would have called a slowcoach and Jim would have called a dither-arse.

Though Jim was friendly with Woody, he would have found him impossible as a colleague. Jim was go-getting and aggressive. He could be selfish, at times impossible. He had divided women into two categories: whores and mothers. The whores knew how to satisfy his lusts, and the mother-substitutes cooked and washed and ironed and provided warmth in bed on cold nights. In spite of the feminist revolution, there were still women who found such men attractive—at least until they'd had a chance to live with them for a month or two.

Woody, unlike Jim, was a shy and sensitive soul. He probably saw women in a purely complementary role. He found them interesting and relaxing as a change from male company, but he would never go out of his way to pursue them. She herself was obviously such a relaxant, and so in her time was Jane. Men like Woody were made for the married life. They were home birds by nature; once settled in a routine they were slow to change. They made ideal partners for sensible women who cared little for the vagaries of fashion and popular culture. Sadly, as Jane had already discovered, they were happy in semi-bachelor bliss, and most of the time they saw no reason to wish for more.

Unlike Jim, Woody was not ambitious; he never reflected on his condition and how it might be improved.

He lacked an eye that might now and again turn inwards and discern what was there and what was not. Once, when she asked him what he made of Sweetman, he said, 'Typical journalist. All periphery. No centre. No hard core.' Come to think of it, the same comment could be applied to Woody himself. When asked for his opinion on a topic in the news, he would tell her what he'd heard from 'a reliable source'. Everything that happened to him took place at two removes away. No immediacy. No personal involvement. *Oratio obliqua* ruled his life. What would he think on his deathbed? Would he say, 'I've had it from a reliable source that my time is up'?

Still, she was fond of him. They were both over fifty, their best years gone for good or ill. In many ways they'd led unsatisfactory lives. He had been disappointed in love not once but twice, while she had found what she thought was happiness, only to discover that she had been living a lie. Given Woody's personal history, it was only natural that he should be suspicious of all women and their wiles. Perhaps he was suspicious even of her. She had spurned him once, and the memory still rankled. He was too proud to force himself upon her. The first move must come from her. He would not budge until he'd received an unambiguous signal. Only then would he rouse himself from his customary inertia.

Of course, his lack of drive and ambition did not matter to her now, not at this stage of her life. She was well off; she did not need a go-getter to support her. In fact she was well able to support both herself and him. He would no longer have any need for what he called 'word-grinding'. They could both retire from the tyranny of the keyboard; they could travel widely, following the sun throughout the year. As that starchy old misery guts T. S. Eliot put it, they would read much of the night, and go south in the winter.

She poured herself another Scotch and settled down to read further in the sex diaries. The question on her mind was whether to let Woody see them. Given his attitude to women, he'd probably be scandalised. For him, women lived on a high-up pedestal, or possibly on a pillar like St Simeon Stylites. Only that could account for his nocturnal torpor. They had kissed each other goodnight and slept in the same bed several times, and never once had he put over a wandering hand in the middle of the night. What on earth would such a man make of Bishop's Delight? The diaries were full of references to it, whatever it was. Quite obviously, some outré sexual position. GUBU, to give it its true title (Grotesque, Unprecedented, Bizarre and Unbelievable). Whatever it was, Jim had been obsessed with it. Otherwise, why should references to it keep recurring throughout the diaries?

> *...longing for another taste of Bishop's Delight all day since morning....*
> *...only Bishop's Delight will cure this heartache....*
> *...today in the Kremlin only the memory of Bishop's Delight kept me sane....*
> *...Hell is within, and Bishop's Delight the only road out to self-forgetfulness....*

What on earth would Woody make of it all? Would he say that Jim had lost his marbles? And what would he think of her, who had lived with such a man for so long? Quite possibly he might wonder about their antics in the marital bed.

In spite of his unsavoury sexual life, she had to admit that Jim had his strong points. For a start, he was more complex than Woody—more imaginative and more original in his thinking. He was convinced that what defined all successful politicians was their protean ability to assume whatever shape or form the occasion demanded. He also told her that the political wind is forever changing, and that a good politician is never caught out facing in the wrong direction. Keen to make people see that he was never to be found in a place where he did not wish to be, he made sure to be conspicuous by his absence as well as by his presence. He was a myth-maker *par excellence*, and in the business of myth-making, the manner of his death was his master stroke. In his death he had posed a question that would never be answered with definitive certainty, at least till the last trump sounded. She would not be surprised if he had hoped to return one day in imitation of those ancient Celtic warriors to lead the country out of ignominious degradation!

She had caught herself out again. He had been such a strong influence on her life that she was still not entirely free. She was living in his shadow, and she would continue to live in his shadow for as long as his sex diaries lived in her imagination. To regain her freedom as a woman, she would have to destroy them. Only then could she achieve everything she had set her heart on. In destroying them she would be risking the condemnation of future historians, but in a real sense she would be doing Jim a good turn. If the diaries were ever published, they would be read mainly by the prurient and the sex-obsessed, and his name would become a byword for outré sex, and she herself would be remembered as the unfortunate wife of a sex maniac. Chauvinistic male historians would blame her for failing in her wifely duty. They would say that she was a prude who knew only of the tedious and unimaginative missionary position, and that her husband, a man of lively and far-reaching imagination, understandably yearned for other possibilities as an escape from the banality of debates at Leinster House.

Furthermore, it was possible that Jim had written his sex diaries as a means of relaxation and wish-fulfilment. They were for his eyes and no one else's. He would have been horrified to think that they had become public property for every gurrier in town to drool over. Besides, there were excellent precedents for the destruction of private papers. Philip Larkin requested on his deathbed that his diaries be destroyed, and Thomas Hardy made several bonfires in the garden of Max Gate to destroy whatever evidence he did not wish preserved for the enjoyment of voyeuristic scholars. The destruction of private papers was no more than a form of editing, a spring-cleaning, a tidying-up before inquisitive posterity could be allowed into the room. If Jim had been given an opportunity, surely he would have requested the destruction of the sex diaries, and she would have done for him what Monica Jones had done for Larkin. In life, Jim was obsessed with his posthumous reputation. He was essentially a private man who washed his dirty linen when no one else was looking.

She found some firelighters, matches and a handful of old newspapers. She put on a headscarf to protect her hair from ash and smoke, got out the brazier from the potting-shed, and started a lively fire in the garden, telling herself that Larkin and Thomas Hardy would have been proud of her. She tore out the pages of the diaries from their binding and watched words like 'pert bottom', 'ripe breasts' and 'Bishop's Delight' being swiftly consumed by fire. The pages blackened and shrivelled, and shreds of ash rose into the air and floated high into the trees. Within half an hour all that was left at the bottom of the brazier was a layer of black ash. Jim was dead. Now she was the only person alive who had heard of Bishop's Delight, undoubtedly a sexual position named after some rascally Renaissance prelate who should never have donned a mitre. Not that it mattered any more. The burning of the diaries was symbolic. The past was dead. She was now free to begin a new life. She would enjoy an Indian summer before winter with its straits and narrows finally set in.

23

Neither winter nor spring brought any change in his routine. He spent two days a week with Anna working on Maguire's papers, and now and again he spent the night at her house. They didn't make love. She just liked to have him lie beside her as she talked about the past in the dark. Once she said that most people in their position would have made love by now, but that lovemaking is sometimes best left to the imagination. 'The physical act is overrated, don't you think? The imagination trumps it every time.'

Slowly but surely, she was devouring him. He had a sense of impotence, both sexual and intellectual, which he'd never experienced before. He wondered if she possessed psychic powers that were undermining his masculinity. There was something weird in the way she looked through him, as if she were in communion with that part of him that remained a locked room to his conscious self. Once he was woken in the small hours by her snoring. The Sacred Heart lamp on the wall cast a red glow on the white quilt under his chin. For a moment he thought he was in hell, or at least somewhere beyond the reach of the living, in the land of the undoubtedly dead. As her snoring grew harsher, he wondered if she were really unaware of her capacity for destruction. She probably saw herself as the victim of a self-absorbed and coldly indifferent man. In a sense she was at once the author and the heroine of one of her own fairy tales. She had been wronged by a wicked wizard called Maguire, and was now awaiting the coming of a hero whose kiss would recall her to life as the beautiful young princess she once was.

In spite of everything, he was convinced that his sufferings served a purpose. By keeping her happy, he would eventually gain access to Maguire's intimate diaries, and living with her had given him insights into Maguire's psychology that he would not otherwise have acquired. His sufferings were but a shadow of those endured by Maguire. Now he knew how the great man must have felt. It was no wonder that he had looked elsewhere for release and consolation. He himself was following in his footsteps, finding strength in the props that formed the furniture of Maguire's restless mind.

He had begun visiting Louise once a week, taking her out to dinner and spending the rest of the evening at her flat. Like Maguire, he enjoyed her company. Hers was a voice of sanity and normality in a world that was leading him down some odd pathways. Not that he minded greatly. He saw his current life as mere smoke in the wind. He was camping on the periphery of a circus ground, watching the winking lights and the comings and goings of the acrobats and artistes and young parents arriving with their excited offspring. Ordinary life with its quiet satisfactions had passed him by. As Louise had reminded him, he and she were outsiders in a world whose aspirations they did not share. If he ever came to be welcomed as an insider, he would soon be rumbled as an impostor.

He continued to meet Sweetman for lunch once a week. Although Sweetman could be a nuisance, and even impossible at times, his acerbic conversation was a change from Anna's continual cud-chewing. Sweetman had fallen out with Louise over the memoir he was supposed to be ghosting. Apparently, she had changed her mind about the kind of story she wished to tell. Unfortunately, she had come across a copy of Rousseau's *Confessions* in the local library, and was taken with his unashamed candour and self-knowledge.

'Kiss-and-tell stories are trashy,' she said. 'I want to write a serious book like Rousseau's. My life has been like no one else's, and I have important things to say about it.'

When Sweetman told her that Rousseau was a man of uncommon intellectual power, and an original thinker to boot, she accused him of implying that she was stupid. One accusation led to another. Sweetman grew hot under the collar and told her to get educated.

'What else could I have said?' he demanded. 'I took on the job thinking I'd get tales of megalopenis, and instead all I got was megalomania.'

'Did you find out anything about Maguire?'

'Not a scrap. We'd only got as far as her schooldays and her hatred of the Sisters of Mercy, her teachers.'

'Surely that could have been interesting!'

'It might have been if she had anything new to say. She sees her convent education as the first of many impediments to the expression of her natural genius. Louise is getting above herself. Still, I didn't like leaving her in the lurch. I'll miss the perks that went with the job.'

The next time Woody went to see Louise she told him that she had decided to write her own memoir, and she asked him to teach her what she called 'style'. She had put him in a difficult position because he could not contemplate a life without her friendship. He couldn't even tell her that it was more than just a matter of 'style'.

'Write the first chapter in your own style, and I'll teach you how to edit it,' he promised.

'You must teach me to write like Rousseau,' she insisted.

'That's impossible. Even I can't write like Rousseau.'

'Teach me to write in your style, then. If you do, I'll be so good to you that you'll never forget it. You have no idea how good I can be.'

That was how their literary collaboration began. As he told himself at the time, it was an offer he could hardly refuse. His life was now divided between Louise and Anna. He spent two evenings a week with each of them; he had only three evenings left for himself. Louise was a willing pupil. As a writer, her besetting sin was prolixity. He bought her a blue pencil and showed her how to cut her first drafts down to the very bone. Within a few months she was a passable subeditor of her own prose. In fact, she cut so ruthlessly that she was in danger of denaturing her pleasantly idiosyncratic style.

'Soon I'll have no need of you,' she boasted. 'But you needn't worry; I'll still be good to you. If I'd had you as my teacher in time, I'd be a fashion columnist for *The Times* by now.'

At one of their Friday meetings, Sweetman told him that MacBride was back in circulation, and that he'd run into him at the Gate Theatre the previous evening. He was looking much reduced, possibly because he was accompanied by his domineering wife, who behaved as if she were *in loco parentis*. When Woody attempted to phone MacBride, it was his wife who took the call.

'Bill isn't well. He isn't seeing journalists any more,' she said.

'I was hoping to talk to him as a friend.'

'He's absent-minded. He may not remember you, which would be embarrassing for him.'

'You needn't worry. I was only hoping to see how he's getting on.'

'He's no longer the man you used to know,' she said. 'He wanders off on his own and then can't remember how to get home. He's a worry for me and the family. Last week he left the house saying he was going out to Bray, and ended up in Portmarnock.'

She was exaggerating, of course. MacBride recognised him at once and invited him into the room he called his study, though as far as he could see there were no books, apart from *Brewer's Dictionary of Phrase and Fable.* On his desk was a copy of *The Irish Echo,* which lay open at the crossword page.

'This is how I spend my time,' he said. 'Maguire thought crosswords were for people who were good for nothing else. How he'd laugh if he knew I'd joined the Dreary Brigade. Listen to this. "Get test for cold." Six letters beginning with "w". Answer "wintry". It's enough to give any serious man the shits. Still, it keeps my mind from seizing up. But I'm gabbling again. What did you come to see me about?'

Woody told him he hadn't come about anything in particular; that he'd just dropped in to see how he was getting on. MacBride poured him a generous glass of Jameson, and treated himself to an equally generous glass of wine.

'I'm at a loose end now,' he said. 'I've lost my business thanks to a careless manager. I haven't got a penny to my name. When I was riding high, I put my property and investments in Maggie's name. Now she watches me like a hawk. She's bossier than Maggie Thatcher ever was. I'm a prisoner in the house I built and paid for. I have all the time in the world on my hands and nothing to do with it. You have no idea what it's like to be in good health and just mooch about all day. I miss Maguire. I go here and there, hoping to run into him. I went to Portmarnock the other day thinking he'd show up. We were both fond of the place for reasons that had nothing to do with golf. Jim couldn't stand golf talk. He used to say that golfers have a brain no bigger than their golf balls. I told Maggie I was going out to Bray, and now she thinks I went to Portmarnock under the impression that it was Bray. The gods are against me. I can't win.'

'So you think Maguire is still alive?'

'I'm sure of it. Jim was too clever to go out in a boat on an empty tank. Don't you fret, he'll be back.'

'Where do you think he is?'

'Paris, where else? I could tell you things about the times we had in Paris together, but I mustn't.... Jim had a high opinion of your writing. When something big was brewing and he wanted to fly a kite, he'd drop you a hint because a hint was all you needed. "That Woody can make a story out of next to nothing," he used to say. He couldn't stand Sweetman, though he never let him see it. He used to call him Cheatman behind his back.'

'If Maguire is in Paris, I'm surprised he hasn't been spotted by now.'

'Jim is an actor and a master of disguise. He had to be, living with Anna. If you're in touch with her, be on your guard. She's a veritable demon. If you're not careful, she'll wring you dry. She was jealous of what Jim and I had in common, and she tried to drive a wedge between us, but Jim saw through her antics and wouldn't stand for any of her meddling. Wives are fine in their place, but now and again men need the company of like-minded men.'

He poured more drinks, then returned to the subject that was uppermost in his mind.

'The crooked timber of humanity is nowhere more apparent than in the Irish character. We're never content unless we're bringing down some noble stag. We can't stand the sight of a man who is greater than ourselves. "He's getting above himself," we shout. "His father was a tinker and his mother was born behind a ditch." We've maligned the greatest Irishman since Dev, and still we're not satisfied. I'll be pleased when this commission that's supposed to be taking evidence finally reports. They won't find anything irregular in my relationship with Jim. That won't stop the gossips, though. What on earth do they want? That's the question you as a journalist should be asking.'

MacBride had seized the opportunity to sound off. After a decent interval, Woody rose to make his escape. MacBride caught him by the sleeve.

'A quick question before you go,' he said. 'Is there anything you and I could do together?'

'What did you have in mind?' Woody asked.

'I'll leave that to you. As a journalist, you must be full of ideas. I know a lot of people. I know things no one else knows. I'm not a spent mackerel, not yet.'

Woody couldn't begin to imagine what was on his mind. 'I'll think about it,' he said.

'We'd be doing each other a good turn,' MacBride said. 'I'd have something to do, and you'd get valuable ammunition for your writing. Besides, we both might enjoy the odd glass along the way.'

'I'm sure there must be something…' Woody said. 'Give me time. I'll be in touch.'

As he cycled home, he went over their conversation in his mind. He couldn't work out what precisely was wrong with MacBride. Admittedly, he was feeling lonely and sorry for himself, which was only to be expected in a newly retired man who'd always led a busy life. He seemed in possession of his mental faculties, and yet there was something odd—something desperate and buttonholing—about his conversation. He was reluctant to get involved with him since he was so busy with Anna and Louise. Perhaps all he was looking for was someone who would listen to him sounding off.

He never did see MacBride again. Six weeks later his wife got up one morning to find him hanging from the sycamore in the back garden. Woody was disturbed by the news. A dead weight of guilt fell on his shoulders. He had misjudged MacBride's condition and had failed to answer his plea for help. His response had been less than humane.

24

Anna, he assumed, had had more than one glass in the kitchen. Over dinner she said that they must be the oddest couple in the country.

'We've known each other for thirty years, we're fond of each other, we go to bed together, but we never make love.'

'We're not very trendy,' he agreed. 'We're more like a couple in a tale of high romance. Do you think there's an imaginary sword between us in the bed?'

'We've fallen into a rut. Abstinence is easier than moderation. There's a lot to be said for a little indulgence now and again. Is it possible that we care too much for each other's feelings?'

That night in bed she put her hand down inside his pyjamas. He lifted her nightdress and drew her towards him.

'Let him rest for a while between my thighs so that I may get used to him little by little as he grows.'

He had read about intercrural intercourse as a form of contraception among primitive peoples, but Anna could hardly be described as primitive. Nonetheless, he did as instructed and waited philosophically for the next move. The lovemaking that followed was like none he had experienced before. Where he had expected firmness, he found flabbiness; where he had expected tautness, he encountered muscular slackness. She lay supine and impassive, receptive rather than active, and when it was all over she emitted a curmurring sound that denoted a pleasure he had not shared. He lay on his back beside her, wondering at the strangeness of his life. Clearly, in the art of loving he had a lot to learn. Both Jane and Louise were younger than Anna, active partners in the business of giving and receiving. He chided himself for having expected too much. With Louise he had already experienced the acme of sexual pleasure. She was ever alert and eager; she would have gained a starred first from Casanova himself. This was his first encounter with middle-aged loving, and it did not bode well for a pleasurable old age.

'That was lovely,' she said. 'I'd forgotten what I was missing. Luckily, we can still make up for lost time.'

She was as good as her word. She had become so addicted to his lovemaking that on Tuesdays and Thursdays they went to bed for an hour in the afternoon because, she said, dinner had a soporific effect on her. She also told him that Maguire had been an indifferent lover, too inclined to fuss over trifles. He would never make love without at least three hours' notice. As a preliminary measure he liked to have a hot bath, and he made her have a bath as well. Even then he was not 100 per cent reliable. Worse still, he had no interest in early morning sex, when most men, she imagined, must be on top form.

'Life is a strange business,' she said. 'It was not Jim's looks that snared me but his soft talk. If I'd married you I'd have led a happier domestic life. I might even have had a family. I've always wanted a boy and a girl. I'd have called the girl Gráinne. I'd have left the naming of the boy to you. What would you have called him?'

'Diarmaid, of course!'

'A brother and sister called Diarmaid and Gráinne? Perhaps it's just as well we never married.'

He did his best to please her for the sake of what one day would become his magnum opus, even when pleasing her went against his natural inclination. There were times when he felt used and put upon, and there were other times when he wondered how he could have been so besotted with her as a young woman. For him at twenty there was no other girl on the planet. He wasn't just besotted: he was obsessed with how she looked, how she carried herself, how she talked and what she said. When she married Maguire he felt that all women were traitors and that he'd never look at another girl again.

Now he saw her as an accusing reminder of his callow youth. She had demolished his idealism at a stroke and put him on the high road to a reductive and cynical perception of life. He was no longer capable of falling selflessly in love; all he could manage was to give something in the hope of receiving at least as much in return. He helped Louise with her memoir in return for sex, and he was doing his best to please Anna to ensure continuing access to what she liked to call 'The Maguire Papers'. Going to bed with her had become part of their unspoken and unwritten contract. More worryingly, it had become part of his sentient, thinking life. Though no longer a practising Catholic, he felt that it balanced the excessive pleasure he found in bed with Louise. That was the kind of theological thinking he could not share with Sweetman, because Sweetman was not the kind of man who dealt in such Augustinian niceties, and neither was Maguire. He flattered himself that he had hit on something. There were two types of men: those who dealt in fine discriminations, and those who didn't. Though he wouldn't mention it to either Anna or Louise, he saw himself as one of the chosen.

In early September, Anna invited him for a week's holiday at her Conamara cottage. 'We'll have fish for dinner every evening,' she said. 'Whatever you catch, I'll cook. Fish is good for the brain. Your prose style will improve beyond your wildest dreams.'

The weather was warm and the sea calm. When he caught more mackerel or pollock than they needed, he exchanged them with other fishermen for whiting, haddock or bass. He was beginning to enjoy the camaraderie of the locals when their idyllic week came to an abrupt end.

They'd spent the morning working in the garden, and in the afternoon they went for a long walk on the cliffs. Coming back, she complained of a headache, and they rested on a rock for a while because she said she felt weak. As soon as they reached home, she lay down while he cooked dinner. He wasn't a first-class cook by any means, but when she vomited after eating he persuaded himself that it was not because of his lack of culinary competence. He suggested an early night, but she wouldn't hear tell of it. She said she'd have a bath, because a hot bath was a restorative that never failed. On the way upstairs she felt dizzy. He ran her bath and helped her to get in. Once immersed she felt much better, and he told her he'd come back in twenty minutes in case she needed him.

The bath had done wonders for her, she said. She came downstairs in her dressing gown and they watched television until bedtime. Against his advice, she had a few whiskies, which she said would make her sleep. In the bedroom she seemed chirpy enough. They didn't make love; she said she'd like to fall asleep with a book in her hand, which was the next best thing. He lay on his back with his eyes closed against the light, while she read a few pages of Ovid's *Metamorphoses*, one of her favourite 'story books'. He was about to drift off when he thought he heard her say something. He imagined she was talking to herself. It was only when she called 'Woody!' that he opened his eyes.

'I can't move my right arm and leg,' she said. 'The book just fell from my hand.'

He got out of bed and pulled back the bedclothes. He lifted her right arm and then her right leg. Both fell limply from his hand. Her left arm and left leg were still all right.

'How do you feel?' he asked.

'My headache's come on again,' she said. 'Maybe you should call Dr Dorian.'

Dorian was attending another patient five miles away, and wouldn't be able to come for at least forty-five minutes. She was lying on her back with her eyes closed and her left arm hanging over the edge of the bed. He raised her arm and placed it across her breast. He was in unchartered territory. He couldn't just sit there waiting for the doctor; he had to do something, and the only thing he could think of was to phone for an ambulance. Afraid that she might go under and that he would be blamed for neglecting her, he kept talking to her to keep her from falling asleep. It was all so unexpected, the transformation in her so sudden and so complete. He felt vulnerable, ignorant and incapable of doing anything to the purpose. At least she was still breathing, and, as his mother would have said, where there's life, there's hope. He kept looking at his watch, praying that either the doctor or the ambulance would come and relieve him of the responsibility that had fallen so heavily on his shoulders.

The doctor was first to arrive. He knew Anna. When she heard his voice, she opened her eyes and smiled with a lopsided twist of the lower lip.

'Don't worry, Anna,' he said. 'We'll get you to hospital. You'll soon be in good hands.'

He tested her right arm and leg, then her left arm and leg. He took her blood pressure and peered into her eyes with a little torch. He took her pulse and listened to her heartbeat. He asked her what she'd been doing, and she told him that she'd had a busy day. He assured her that her speech was all right and that it was nothing too serious—not a stroke. She'd been overdoing things; she'd had a muscular spasm and would be back on her feet in a day or two, he promised. She tried to smile with the good side of her face, and raised her good arm momentarily from the coverlet before letting it drop again.

Shortly afterwards the ambulance arrived. Dr Dorian told the paramedics what was required, and gave them instructions to which they listened as if they'd heard them many times before. On the way to the hospital in Galway, Woody sat beside the gurney caressing the back of her hand with his thumb, repeating her name in an effort to hold her attention. She seemed to be sleeping, but still he persisted because he felt that he should be doing or saying something all the time. Most of what he said was no more than gabbling, but at least it was something, because he sensed that if he should stop even for a moment she might slip out of his life, never to return. To complicate matters, he felt guilty. Should he not have taken a more firm stand? Her sister Lily would blame him for not putting his foot down. She was not to know that Anna was incorrigible; that single malt was her daily fuel and that no one could stand between her and her 'wee dram'. He was running out of things to say. He wanted to speak words of comfort, but when spoken they sounded hollow on his tongue. He pressed her hand and told her how much he loved her, but there was no corresponding pressure from hers. The falsity of his words shocked him. He longed to be a simple man like his father, a countryman with only one moral register, who said what he meant and never had occasion to say anything else. He was suffering agonies of self-scrutiny when he remembered Sweetman and knew at once that at least Sweetman would not have acquitted himself any better. He kept patting her hand and telling her about all the things they'd do together when she recovered. It was such a travesty of the truth that he kept wincing at the sound of his own words. Once he thought he felt a tremor of response in her fingers, but he could not be sure. It was all so agonising, and possibly so futile, because if she could not hear him, what was the point of talking to her, yet he had to persist for his own sake if not for hers.

Nothing in his life had prepared him for this moment. They'd been together for not much more than a year. He knew Jane and Louise much better than he did Anna. In a similar situation with either of them he would know how to behave as a matter of instinct. He would not have to ask himself how he was doing, and then wonder if perhaps his behaviour was somehow awry. It was all so wrong. His whole life was wrong. It had gone out of plumb the day Jane left him, and now there was no hope of ever recovering the perpendicular.

In the hospital he waited while the consultant and doctors did their tests. After an hour that seemed like three, the consultant told him that Anna's brain had been seriously damaged by a haemorrhage and that she would never recover full use of her limbs and mental powers. He sat by her bed, unable to think. She was in deep coma, no longer conscious of her surroundings. He stretched his legs and closed his eyes.

In the morning he phoned her sister Lily in Skibbereen.

'When did all this happen?' she asked.

'Last night. She was admitted to hospital at eleven.'

'Then I should have been told at eleven,' she snapped.

'I was busy looking after Anna. She was my first concern.'

Lily lost no time in getting to Galway. Shortly after two in the afternoon, she burst through the swing doors of the ward. Tall, buxom and commanding, she strutted rather than walked. She pointedly ignored Woody's hesitant presence and grasped Anna's left hand. She placed her other hand on Anna's forehead and fleetingly touched her cheek.

'Anna's life is in danger. If we don't act now she'll slip away before our very eyes,' she declared.

Next, she beckoned to a passing nurse. When the nurse ignored her, she turned to Woody. 'Who's in charge here? We need to make things happen or Anna will be a goner.'

'The consultant saw her early this morning and the house doctor has been to see her twice since then. They're doing as much as they can in the circumstances.'

'Are you a doctor?'

'No, but I'm a close friend of Anna.'

'She was always a great one for making friends. She was forever picking up waifs and strays.' She gazed at him for more than a moment as if trying to divine whether he was a waif or merely a stray.

She picked up the patient's chart at the end of the bed and studied it for a split second.

'Gobbledegook to confuse the public!' she pronounced. 'My husband died of cancer two years ago. His chart looked exactly the same.'

A nurse approached and took Anna's blood pressure and temperature.

'I'd like to speak to the patient's consultant,' Lily said.

'Mr Bradley will be doing his rounds at eight o'clock tomorrow morning,' the nurse replied. 'You'll be able to speak to him then.'

'I'd like to speak to him now,' Lily said.

'That's impossible. Mr Bradley sees his patients twice a day, at eight in the morning and again at four in the afternoon.'

'But what if my sister dies in the meantime?'

'I don't know the answer to that question, I'm afraid.'

The nurse left them, and Woody sat down out of sheer exhaustion.

'You look a total wreck, Mr Woody. What you need is a good night's sleep. Why don't you go home and let me keep watch over Anna? You can come back in the morning looking much better, I hope.'

Woody thanked her for being so thoughtful, though he felt that what she really needed was a striker's kick up what Sweetman called the fundamental orifice. She was the very antithesis of Anna, who was both refined and fine-boned. He wondered for a moment if she was an impostor or, worse, a jealous stepsister. It was hard to imagine how two full sisters could differ so much in personality, behaviour and sensibility.

He felt relieved at having made his escape. He went to the nearest pub and ordered a Jameson and a pint of Guinness, which he took to a table in the corner farthest from the other customers. He'd had a testing week, and Lily had put the tin hat on it, as Jane would have said. He longed to talk to a solid, sensible woman capable of offering sympathy and comfort, but Jane wouldn't understand, and anyway, both she and Louise were three hours' drive away. There was nothing for it but to take a taxi back to the cottage and eat at the village fish and chip shop. He would have an early night, think of Anna, and try to forget about Lily for at least twelve hours.

25

He went back to the hospital the following morning at eleven. Lily was sitting by the bedside, holding Anna's hand. She looked him up and down as if trying to recall who he might be. When he enquired about the patient she said that Anna was in God's hands, which was just as well since house doctors these days were young harum-scarums who could not be trusted to get anything right. He asked if she'd had breakfast, and she said she'd had a biscuit.

'I'll relieve you if you like while you go out to eat.'

'Relieve me? There's no relief for me while Anna's life is in danger. She's my only sister. We were always close, as only sisters can be.'

'If you like I'll go out and get you something. What would you like?'

'A bowl of hot porridge with honey and raisins would be nice, but since that's impossible I'll have a ham and tomato sandwich, an orange, a Kit-Kat, and some coffee to keep my strength up. I must stay here with Anna in her hour of need.'

Forty-five minutes later he came back fully provisioned. He had even brought her paper napkins, which she said were in excess of requirements since she never went anywhere without her own supply. He sat by the bedside as she ate, conscious that his presence was no longer required. Anna did not look like Anna: her puffy face had lost all trace of its former character. It was a likeness left behind by a departed spirit, a feeble reminder of her once animated self.

'Anna's life was a tragedy from start to finish,' Lily said.

'She's a highly gifted writer,' he reminded her. 'She has a new book coming out in the spring. I hope she's feeling better by then.' He felt uneasy talking about Anna while she lay unconscious beside them, but Lily did not suffer from any such qualms.

'Anna was a poor judge of men. She attracted all sorts of oddballs. Not one solid man among the lot of them.'

'Maybe she liked oddballs, if by oddballs you mean gifted men of distinctive character. Not every woman can boast of having married a Taoiseach.'

'Give me a no-nonsense man, and I'll show you a man who is true to his wife. Anna was taken in by cleverness. Journalists, writers, actors, politicians—they're all like smoke from a chimney, there one minute and gone the next.' She looked at him as if he might vanish in a puff of smoke at any moment.

He felt distinctly uncomfortable. 'It's nearly lunchtime,' he said. 'I'd better go and find something to eat. I'll be back shortly.'

'You needn't worry. I'll be here. I'm digging myself in for a long vigil.'

He had a pub lunch, a steak and kidney pie and a pint of Guinness, followed by rhubarb crumble and a glass of the house red. Anna would be proud of him for mixing his drinks. 'A man who laughs at old wives' tales and lower-middle-class shibboleths is a man after my own heart,' she'd say. 'I come from strong stock that never wilted.' Lily came from the same strong stock, but in her case strength manifested itself as small-minded prejudice. He'd had enough of her ranting. He did the rounds of the bookshops. In each he went to the children's section where he looked through Anna's books, not because he was interested in children's literature but because he needed to remember her and feel that he once knew her.

As he climbed the steps to the hospital entrance the following morning, he met Lily coming down.

'You're late, Mr Woody,' she said. 'She died at 7.03 this morning. I sat with her till the end, holding her hand, reminding her of the childhood games we used to play together. It was a lovely death, gentle and touching to watch, like a mute swan drifting downriver.'

'I'm sorry,' he said.

'You can relax now. I'll take care of everything. I buried my husband not so long ago. I know what needs to be done and how to do it.'

'I'd better give you my address and mobile number, in case you wish to get in touch with me.'

'There's no need for fuss. Details of the death and funeral arrangements will be published in *The Irish Times*. Everything will be done as Anna would have wished.'

He felt like saying, 'Fuck off, you bitch!' Instead he said, 'Best of luck. You look a wreck after your vigil. I'm sure you could do with a hot bath and a good night's sleep.'

He drove to the cottage to pick up his things. Then, remembering that he had a key to Anna's residence in Howth, he drove back to Dublin without losing any time. His first thought was to get there before Lily and pick up his papers and laptop, and anything else of relevance he might discover. The study was as he'd left it, his notes still on the desk. He had been through what might be called Maguire's official journal; now he needed to find his sex diary before someone else did. The most likely repository for such a precious document was Anna's study, which he'd only seen from the door. In a surge of excitement he raced up the stairs. He looked in all the obvious places: in her desk, in her bookcase, and in the four cardboard boxes that were stacked in a corner, only to be disappointed. Behind the chaise longue was an arched alcove with two bookshelves above and a heavy safe below. It was an ancient safe, which raised his hopes. He went to her desk again, looking for the key, but all he found was a key to the desk drawers. He searched her bedroom, but the only items relevant to Maguire's sexual tastes were two pairs of crotchless green knickers, which he placed under a pillow for Lily to moralise over. He felt certain that the personal diaries must be in the safe, and he felt equally certain that if Lily found them first she would see them as a threat to public morality and destroy them.

Breaking into the safe was not an immediate possibility. There was nothing further he could do, short of engaging the services of a member of the criminal fraternity, thereby putting his professional career at risk. He went downstairs to the study and surveyed what was left of Maguire's single malts. He and Anna had got through most of them. All that remained was a bottle of Balvenie and a bottle of Talisker. He put the Talisker in his rucksack for future reference, and poured himself a shot of the Balvenie. He sat behind Maguire's desk, savouring his whisky and thinking of how abruptly a chapter of his life had ended. He would miss Anna. At times he had found her a nuisance, but she was a kindly soul, and she made quirky conversation of a kind he found entertaining.

He was enjoying the Balvenie, and it occurred to him that Anna would have wished him to enjoy the rest of the bottle in the privacy of his own home. He placed it in his rucksack with his papers and the Talisker, which he carried out to the car. He returned for his laptop and looked around the study one last time. It was late in the evening; shadows were beginning to fill empty corners. He felt weary after the drive. He wondered how he'd ever found the energy to do so much work on the biography. Tomorrow he'd feel stronger. He'd write Anna's obituary, and he would take care to write something personal that no other journalist was capable of writing.

When he phoned the editor of *The Irish Times* the following morning, he was told that Lily had already been in touch with them and that an obituary had been written.

'I wasn't planning to write a formal obit,' he explained. 'What I'd like to write is a light-hearted piece of reminiscence, something of a personal nature that no one else could write.'

'Then write it for the diary column. There's no news like people news.'

He was delighted to be given an opportunity to take some of the wind out of Lily's sails. He would do Anna's quirky sense of humour full justice, while sailing as close to the wind as good taste permitted—anything to discomfit her bitch of a sister.

Lily had made the funeral into an occasion to glorify her own family. They turned out in force, as did Maguire's former political colleagues. There was a whiff of the countryside about the service; the readings were not those Anna would have chosen, and the hymns were those sung in rural parishes rather than by cathedral choirs. Woody sat at the back of the church wondering what Anna would have made of it all. She was not a churchgoer. The pious old lady the priest spoke of bore little resemblance to the Anna he knew. When it was all over, he slipped away without waiting to make his presence known. It was a banal ending to one of the more offbeat episodes of his life.

Two months later he had a letter from Anna's solicitor letting him know that she had bequeathed him her cottage in Conamara and ownership of the copyright of her published and unpublished works, as well as any income derived from them. She had left her investments and both her houses to Lily, and she had donated Maguire's papers to the National Library. He felt humbled by her generosity, and overjoyed when he discovered that the annual income from her books far exceeded his own income from writing. Now he could afford to relax, lay off journalism for a while and devote himself to the serious business of Maguire's biography, which must have been what Anna had intended.

As winter approached, he fancied a break before the months of darkness set in. He couldn't face a sad little holiday abroad on his own, and he wondered if he should phone Jane to see if she had forgiven him. He agonised uncertainly for a week. Then, in a moment of unaccustomed self-confidence, he invited her out to dinner. On the phone she seemed her usual bubbly self. She had obviously forgiven him everything. They met in one of their old haunts. He told her about Anna's death and his unexpected good fortune.

'I've got good news for you as well,' she smiled. 'I'm getting married in April.'

'Congratulations!' he said, putting on his actor's voice. 'Do I know the lucky man?'

'Probably not. He was directing traffic on O'Connell Bridge when I spotted him. He's my next door neighbour from home.'

'Another Aran Islander!'

'We're two of a kind, simple souls at sea in the city. We're both victims of different shipwrecks, hoping to reach land together one day.' She smiled and reached across the table for his hand.

'You used to say that all you need is money, and to rile you, I used to say all you need is love. In a curious way we both got our wish,' she said.

She had made him feel foolish. For a moment he suspected that she must see him as the shallowest of men.

'You and I had some good times,' she smiled. 'I learned a lot from you, Woody. I was an innocent when I met you. I used to read the newspapers and marvel at how clever they were. Now I question everything I read and hear.'

'Don't question your husband too closely. He mightn't like it.'

'Don't worry, you've taught me about men as well. All they need to be happy is plenty of good food and flattery.'

As they parted, he kissed her cheek. She kissed him on the lips and smiled. 'Who knows, our paths may cross again one day.'

He went home despondent. In talking to her he discovered that he was still in love with her. He poured himself a glass of Maguire's Balvenie and asked himself where he had gone wrong. 'To snare a woman, you need to be a salesman,' he said aloud. 'It doesn't matter what you're selling; if you're a good salesman, you'll sell it.' He held up his glass to the light before lowering it to his lips.

Open-collared honesty—that was his undoing. He'd let her peer into his mind. He'd stood naked before her; he'd let her see too much. His training had taught him to be clear and concise, to give the reader the picture at a glance, whereas in love, as in politics, dissembling and obfuscation took the prize. He was so true to himself that she'd seen right through him, while her policeman had had enough peasant cunning to cover up his game. It was a tragedy, not just for him personally but for Jane as well. She said he'd taught her scepticism. He should have taught her never to trust a man in big boots.

He'd learnt one or two things from her. Love, like religion, thrived on mystery and mystique, which when all was said and done meant keeping up the illusion that Celia never shits. He had come to the end of the Balvenie. Mercifully, he could rely on the Talisker for another day or two.

26

The commission looking into the circumstances of Maguire's death reported the following summer, over three years after the event. As might be expected, the document it produced was longwinded and exhausting, if not as exhaustive as expected. It considered an impressive range of theories, including those invented by imaginative journalists in search of notoriety and personal advantage. Finally, it came down on the side of the plodders who had believed all along that the death of the Taoiseach was an unfortunate accident. As members of the commission saw things, Maguire had taken his boat out for a day's fishing. He ran out of petrol and panicked at the thought of drifting out of sight of land. He tried to swim ashore and failed in the attempt. His body was carried out to sea and never seen again. The commission had no answer to the question of the missing oars, which, it said, pointed to the absence of a third party since a third party would have made certain to cover its tracks and not to do anything that might point to foul play.

Sweetman was the first to comment on the commission's report in his evening TV news programme. He said that he'd read every tautological word of it and had come to the conclusion that it was all an expensive whitewash. It considered a range of unlikely theories and rightly rejected them, while ignoring those that the establishment would rather forget. The morning newspapers followed suit and took the same predictable view. The long-awaited report had been a waste of time and taxpayers' money. One journalist said that it had failed to consider the most obvious theory of all: that Maguire, during the Northern Ireland negotiations, had been in the British government's pocket and had paid the price of his perfidy with his life. Even Sweetman didn't go that far. He said that Maguire had presided over twelve years of unprecedented prosperity. His time was a golden age in which everyone lived for the day without a thought for tomorrow. The golden age had come to an end, and Maguire in his wisdom had seen the shadow of Nemesis on the horizon and had left the stage while the audience was still clapping and before the booing had time to start. Now he was probably enjoying the demimonde of Paris in disguise and disposing of the ample funds he had amassed in office.

Woody wrote an ironic piece, congratulating the commission on its elephantine gestation while marvelling at the triviality of the result. Predictably, the commission's report did little to satisfy the public's taste for skulduggery and conspiracy. Everyone who could read a newspaper firmly believed that there was more to Maguire's disappearance than the government wanted them to know. The whole seemingly shady business was still a hot topic of debate in every pub and living room in the country.

Sweetman gloried in the hoo-ha. As he said to Woody, 'It's all grist to our mill. Even if there's no truth in any of the conspiracy theories, there's a story in refuting them. We make our living from assertion and rebuttal, to be followed inevitably by further assertion and further rebuttal. We may run out of new ideas but we'll never run out of copy.'

Sweetman's biography, *Death of a Taoiseach*, published three years after Maguire's disappearance, was both a critical and commercial success. In his journalism he had made sure that interest in Maguire remained alive, and his book, which was serialised in the press, attracted favourable reviews from academics and fellow journalists alike. Woody had expected a hastily assembled mishmash of fact and fiction. Instead, his book was a surprisingly competent assessment of Maguire's public and private lives. It was forthright and provocative, presenting Maguire as a prodigiously gifted man who was deeply flawed in his sexuality. He argued that Maguire's remote and at times glacial public persona was not the real man at all, and that the effort of hiding behind his mask forced him to compensate by relaxing on occasion with women who were less fastidious than his puritanical Irish wife. Hence his love of Paris. After all, he had admitted that his favourite French paintings were Ingres's *La Grande Baigneuse* and Gauguin's *Manao Tupapau*, both of which showed a young woman in the nude.

Woody read the biography as a man with a vested interest in the subject. He could not help admiring the ease with which the thing was done, but as he came to the last paragraph he said to himself, 'I must not follow in Sweetman's footsteps. Like every other biographer I've ever read, he's fully convinced that there's a reason for everything, and consequently he has an explanation for everything. He makes no allowance for chance and contingency, twin forces capable of defeating the strongest human will.' Sweetman was a novelist manqué who thought he could shape his great work as he pleased without sacrificing a word of the truth. Maguire put it differently in his diaries: 'When things come right, we say we planned them. When they go wrong, we blame sod's law.'

Sweetman didn't seem to know that we are all walking mysteries; that the human heart is by nature perverse, deceitful and desperately wicked. Jane would have told him to read Jeremiah: 'They were as fed horses in the morning: everyone neighing after his neighbour's wife.' Maguire was only running true to form; there was nothing unusual in his sexuality.

As he expected, Sweetman was vain enough to think that he had captured Maguire in the flesh as a lepidopterist might net a rare butterfly. Maguire was not so easily accounted for. His protean nature made him a cynic one moment and humanely generous the next. In the space of an afternoon he could be exuberant, reflective, modest, and insufferably big-headed. One day he would say that in politics stupidity was no handicap, and on the next argue that success in politics was the very pinnacle of human achievement.

'The stakes are high,' he'd claim. 'We are contending for nothing less than a permanent place in history and our only weapons are our gifts of judgement, persuasion and leadership. The politician who walks in someone else's tracks leaves no footprints behind him.' On other occasions he could be engagingly irresponsible. He once told Woody over a drink that a good blowjob was more satisfying than the most resounding political victory.

So where was the true Maguire to be found? Not in Sweetman's reductive pages, and certainly not in Maguire's own journal and sex diary. He himself was writing a critical biography, though he knew that he could never capture the living man in all his contradictions. Biography, like autobiography, was flawed at conception. In human affairs there was no absolute and no stability. All was flux and changing perceptions, yours, mine, his and hers, one seeking to challenge and refute the others. In the coming years all he himself could do was to produce a book that showed Maguire in a light that had not been cast on him before. He would paint him as a fully rounded man, a scholar as well as political tactician, capable of friendship as well as robust rivalry, not entirely at ease in a country of rain and small-minded gossips. Had he been born in the warm south, he might have found fulfilment.

He dropped all work on his magnum opus for the time being and devoted his leisure hours to helping Louise with her Rousseau-inspired memoir. It seemed to him that she was barking up the wrong tree, but that was something she would have to discover for herself. When they had come to the end of their labours, she insisted on the title *Love Conquers All*. He tried to tell her that it wasn't suitable, but she wouldn't listen. They sent out the text to seven publishers. The only one who responded said that as a book it fell between two stools, while omitting to name the stools. Louise was inconsolable. When he tried to reason with her she told him she didn't need a comforter.

'The Beetles were wrong and Maguire was right,' she said. 'He used to say that all you need is sex.'

'It's certainly true in books,' Woody said. 'If you give me carte blanche to rewrite your memoir, I promise you it will be published.'

'Fire away,' she said, 'but you won't publish it under my name.'

'Let me think about it,' he said. 'This is an artistic problem, and like all artistic problems it won't be solved by mere reasoning.'

'Then how will it be solved?'

'By a happy conjunction of chance and intuition. Imagination, not love, conquers all.'

'Promises, promises. You journalists are all the same.'

He could see that she was disappointed in him; he knew he had let her down. 'Give me six months,' he said. 'I won't come back till I have a finished typescript to place in your hand.'

He was annoyed with himself, so annoyed that he was determined to prove her wrong. He read her memoir again, and saw that like all real lives it lacked shape. If he imposed on it a shape of his own, it would no longer be the life she thought she'd led. He ran his eye along his bookshelves and took down John Cleland's *Memoirs of a Woman of Pleasure*. Quite unwittingly, he had stumbled on his template: he would write a novel based on her memoir while giving no indication of his true intention. It would be a seductive novel written from the point of view of a woman who found meaning and pleasure in giving sexual delight to men. She would answer to male fantasies of the perfect woman, and would be so gifted in turning the tables on men that the reservations of women readers would be transformed to admiration of her wit and repartee. Of course, he wouldn't say any of that to Louise. He would hand her the typescript and bask in her surprise and delight.

Every weekend he went over to Galway to enjoy the peace of the cottage Anna had left him. It wasn't perfect peace because of the screaming seagulls that came to perch on his roof-ridge every afternoon. They reminded him of the agitated world of words-for-profit he had left behind in Dublin as opposed to the perfect world of male fantasy he was seeking to create. Whenever his imagination flagged he was tempted to go back to Louise for inspiration, but against the odds he carried on doggedly to the end. Working at weekends only, he wrote the novel in six months, and spent another month polishing what he'd written. He felt so pleased with his prose that he thought he might spring a surprise.

He didn't phone her to let her know he was coming. He arrived expectantly at her flat one Saturday morning with the typescript in his bag. A woman whom he took for the cleaner opened the door. He was about to ask if Louise was at home when she reached out and grasped his hand.

'Come in, Woody. I know you won't believe it but I'm Louise.'

She led him to the sofa and told him that she'd had an operation for gallstones that went badly wrong. She was much reduced. She looked pale and worn, her youthful bloom quite gone. Though her dark eyes had lost some of their dazzle, they were all that reminded him of the girl he used to know. He was so shocked by her appearance that he realised he must drop everything else and take care of her. The typescript in his bag was no longer of any account.

He asked if he could make her a cup of tea, and she said she hadn't had lunch and that she fancied fish and chips because she hadn't had any fish in the hospital. By the time he returned with the fish and chips and a bottle of wine, she had done her hair and put on some make-up. She looked less ghostlike, almost human again.

'You should have got in touch with me,' he said.

'We made a bargain. I knew you'd come back some time, but I didn't know when.'

'If I'd known you were unwell I'd have come right away.'

'I'm an awkward girl, and you're an awkward boy. We're two of a kind.'

She told him about her operation, which she'd been assured was just a routine affair. Something had gone wrong; she didn't know what, but she suspected the surgeon must have cut something he shouldn't have cut, resulting in a damaged bile duct.

'My father used to work in a hospital,' she said. 'He had no time for surgeons. His advice was, "Never trust a man with a knife." '

He reached for her hand, realising that in her vulnerability she had become precious to him. She had no more than half a glass of wine, what she called a taste, but it seemed to lift her spirits. The afternoon gradually faded into evening, and when he asked her what she'd like for dinner she said she felt so weak that she had better go to bed.

'It's funny in a way,' she smiled wanly. 'Going to bed has taken on a completely new meaning for me.'

'Why don't we go down to the cottage for a week or two? The fresh sea air will do you good.'

'What about your work?'

'We needn't worry about that. It will still be there when we come back.'

For the first few days she seemed fragile and unsteady. They spent the mornings sitting in the garden. Sometimes he would read to her, mainly short stories by Katherine Mansfield, whose writing she seemed to enjoy. Gradually, her strength returned, and one afternoon she said she'd like to go for a short walk. He led her to the seat on the cliff facing west. They sat looking in silence at the hazy horizon, watching a boat going down the bay. The boat moved slowly, almost imperceptibly. Here was a life where everything happened at a snail's pace. The sun was going down behind a straggle of inky-blue-black-crimson clouds, a mixture of conflicting colours that no conventional artist would have chosen. There was a faint suggestion of incongruity and business that was not entirely above board.

'How do you feel now?' he asked.

'Worn out, as if I'd been around for six hundred years.'

'That makes two of us. I often think that life is longer than we've been led to believe.'

'I hope you're not tiring of it all!'

'No, I was thinking that you and I should get together. I have a three-bedroom house, big enough for both of us. We could have a bedroom each to ourselves, and make the spare bedroom our rump-room for playing in.'

'You beast, Woody! But isn't that why I'm so fond of you?!' She gave him a dig in the ribs.

'You must have liked Maguire as well.'

'He put pressure on me. You didn't. I've always enjoyed your sense of fun. Once or twice you made me feel we were lovers.'

'Well, maybe we were. These things are to do with the imagination, not the body.'

'But the body does come into it. It gets the imagination going.'

'That's settled, then. Neither of us can see any impediment to our living together.'

He put an arm around her shoulders, and she turned and kissed him. For a while they sat in silence, looking out at an indefinable merging of sky and sea.

'Why do you like Katherine Mansfield?' he asked at length.

'Because I feel I know her. At times I feel she's been through the same hoop I've been through. I know she hasn't, but she seems to know what it's been like for me.'

'She wasn't like you at all. She wasn't an easy woman to love. Everyone who knew her, including her husband, Middleton Murry, came off second best.'

'And so they should,' she said.

He longed for a second chance, to have her by his side as she was when he first met her. Life was so tantalising in its imperfection. Always the near miss. Never the time and the place and the loved one as she once was, all together.

'I'm sorry, Woody,' she said. 'I wish I were feeling stronger.'

'We're both past our best, but it doesn't matter. We still remember each other as we used to be.'

'You make me feel guilty. I'd like to be young for you again. I've wasted my life on futile dreams.'

'No dream is futile. Our dreams keep us going; they express our idea of perfection. That sunset sums it up. Not quite perfect, but still unlike any sunset I've ever seen.'

'I'm just pleased to be here to see it.'

'Tell me, Louise. Was there ever such a thing as Bishop's Delight?'

'Why do you ask?'

'There's a reference to it in one of Maguire's diaries. I just wondered what it could be.'

'Maguire was a joker. It was his nickname for me. He thought it funny that I should have a bishop for a friend.'

'So I have been enjoying Bishop's Delight without knowing it.'

'And with any luck you'll enjoy it again. It's nothing in particular. Only the way I do things, I suppose.'

'Nothing in particular! It's everything, Louise. *Everything.*'